CITY SHIFTERS: THE PRIDE

BOOK 4

Cut to the Chase

LAYLA NASH

Cover design by
Resplendent Media

Interior book design by
Write Dream Repeat Book Design LLC

chapter 1

I walked into the Council offices well after dark during the busiest time of night for the bar. I needed to be there, supervising the pack before they started tearing things up, but I'd heard hide nor hair from the other wolf pack in the city until just a few hours earlier. I didn't trust Miles Evershaw even the slightest bit, but sometimes the man had good ideas. If he reached out directly to me rather than through the Council intermediaries, he had his reasons.

Light spilled from only one doorway in the dark hall, and I found Evershaw waiting in the SilverLine pack office. He read from a thick book, a history of something boring no doubt, but rose as I walked in. "O'Shea. Thank you for coming."

"What's up, Evershaw?" I sauntered in like it was my office and he was the interloper, and dragged my fingers along the back of a fancy leather couch – leaving my scent behind to drive him nuts later. "Where's your minion?"

"Todd?" Evershaw set the book aside as he watched me, the corner of his mouth turning up. The touch of gray at his temples made him look distinguished rather than old, but his real age showed in his eyes. Haunted. The other alpha poured a glass of whiskey. "He's on a date, actually." He snorted, shaking his head. "Imagine. Who has time to date?"

"No joke." I took the glass he offered, pausing only to inhale the warm whiskey scent before sipping. At least Evershaw believed in spending money on the things that mattered – comfortable furniture and good liquor.

Evershaw poured for himself, and then gestured at the couch and the seat he'd previously occupied. "Sit for a moment, O'Shea."

I did, a hint of uneasiness bubbling up in my stomach. We'd never been in a room this long without threatening each other. The other shoe would drop eventually. The buttery leather creaked as I adjusted my legs, the high-heeled boot revealed as my jeans rode up. He studied it for a long moment, a hint of consideration in his expression, but I refused to adjust my jeans. Couldn't show weakness or hesitation, especially in front of him.

Evershaw swirled the whiskey in his glass, though his blue eyes remained on me. "I won't beat around the bush, O'Shea. Neither of us has time to search for a mate. With the way this Council is going, the wolves need to establish an agreement to protect us from the felines and the other riffraff. The best way to do that is to combine our packs. You and I mate, and lead together."

I blinked, staring at him. Waiting for a logical response.

Nothing occurred to me.

His eyebrows arched. "Well?"

"You can't be serious."

"Oh, I am." Evershaw watched me with his damnably blank expression. "There is no wolf in this city with the balls to ask you out, much less mate you, O'Shea. Unless you're hunting for a guy outside the city – and I know you're not, because all you do is work – you're never going to get a mate. Never going to whelp some pups."

"Not every woman wants kids, Evershaw. Check your judgments."

"Fine. But you also haven't been on a date in years. This is an easy solution, O'Shea."

My foot bounced again as I sipped the whiskey, needing a little liquid courage. I could cut the man down when he was being an ass or challenging me in front of my pack, but when he tried to hold a normal conversation, he put me completely off-balance. Which was no doubt his goal. "Easy solution for you, maybe. But I don't feel like giving up my pack, Evershaw."

"We combine packs. You and I will be in charge." His long fingers drummed on the arm of his chair. "My pack is not accustomed to shared alphas. It will take some adjustment."

"And what about Rafe?" I studied the glass of whiskey, stunned that I was actually halfway considering it. Evershaw offered a practical, simple solution to several different problems in my life. I wanted a mate, and eventually children, and someone to be my partner – but the other alpha was right. Very few men in the city would dare ask me out. He was an asshole, but if we established ground rules before getting married, maybe...

"I don't give a shit what Rafe does." Evershaw got up and retrieved the bottle, splashing more whiskey into his glass before topping mine off. "But unless he's ready to be a beta, he's not staying in my pack."

"He's my brother." I plucked at a loose thread on my jeans. "Which is why it would never work with us, Evershaw. Not just because I don't like you and find the idea of fucking you off-putting, but because you have no respect for family."

"Off-putting?" He definitely smiled, though he hid it quickly. "You must suffer from a lack of imagination or experience, Ruby. Something we can correct immediately."

My wolf bristled but I refused to react, only raising my eyebrows as I studied him. I took refuge in disdain, wrapping myself up in the chilly demeanor that had protected me all the way to being alpha of my own pack. "Evershaw, you're on dangerous territory."

"Very well. I'm not going to beg you, O'Shea. But this agreement has an expiration date. I'll give you a week to consider it, and expect your answer then."

"You have your answer now. I'm not going to mate with you, and I'm sure as hell not going to let you take over my pack."

Those cold blue eyes watched me as I downed the rest of the whiskey and stood, leaving the glass on the small end table. I straightened my leather jacket as I looked down at where he sprawled in the chair.

Evershaw glanced at his phone as it chimed, but when I turned to go his voice stopped me in my tracks. "I'm the only man in this city who understands you, Ruby. You might not like me very much, but at least I respect you. I know what it means to be alpha. I understand the pressure, the burdens, the demands. I respect what you've been able to accomplish. And I happen to think we would make very strong, very attractive children. Think about it."

I stared at the door, glad my back was to him as his words punched through my chest. Maybe he was right. For half a second, I considered turning back, getting more whiskey, and letting him talk me into sampling the wares. It had been at least a year since I'd had sex, and regardless of Evershaw's technique, a strong breeze would probably be enough to get me off. I gritted my teeth and strode out the door without looking back.

chapter 2

Carter sat at the bar at O'Shea's, nursing a beer as he watched everything going on behind him in the mirror. He didn't want to go back to the house. Between Logan and Natalia, Benedict and Eloise, and Atticus and Sophia, the mansion had turned into date night every night. Carter made a face and reached for another handful of peanuts. He was happy for them, of course, but that didn't make seeing the lovey-dovey cuddling and murmuring and kissing easy. Especially since he still didn't have the same.

A commotion made him look up, and Ruby O'Shea tore into the bar with a ferocious snarl on her face. She slammed the door and strode toward the bar without looking at anyone. The pack members who lounged around the pool table cringed low in their seats and then slunk to the door. The humans populating the bar looked around, uncomfortable, then started asking for the check. Even if they didn't know O'Shea's was a pack bar full of shifters, the humans sensed the tension.

Carter raised his beer to drink, trying to hide a smile as Ruby went behind the bar and started yanking bottles down left and right. He waited until a bottle of tequila landed on the bar in front of him before he cleared his throat. "Rough day?"

She shot him a dark look. "Don't start with me, Chase."

He just smiled. "Come on, Ruby. You're not going to scare me."

Her teeth and a couple of her piercings shone in the light as she ducked to retrieve something from under the bar, then smacked a pair of limes down in front of him. A knife flashed and she had several wedges ready, along with a saltshaker. She leveled the blade at him. "You want to stay and crack jokes, Carter? Then you drink."

"Line 'em up." He uncapped the bottle of tequila and filled the shot glasses as she set them out, and though he had no problem holding his liquor, he got a little nervous as the number of glasses reached into the double digits. "I just went on the third terrible date this week, so you'll have to work to beat that."

Her dark eyes narrowed and she licked the side of her hand, pouring salt onto it before handing him the shaker. "Worst first and last date ever. Propositioned as a business deal. Since no other man in the entire city would ever ask me out."

Carter winced. "Ouch."

"Yeah." She licked the salt off her hand, tossed back a shot of tequila, and bit into a lime. He followed, the tequila burning his nose and throat and making him blink, as he turned on the stool to watch while she snapped orders at the few pack members that remained.

When she returned, he caught her wrist. "Hey. You're killing business down here. Let's go upstairs."

"This is my bar, I'll kill business if I want."

It wasn't bravado. Something else bothered her, he could tell. Something to do with that whole 'no man would ask her out' thing, and that was too serious for her to admit in a public place, where her pack might sense weakness. Carter started pouring the shots back into the bottle. "You're too good of a businesswoman to do that. Seriously. Jules and the guys can handle things down here, and Rafe is out for the night. We can go upstairs and I'll tell you all about my awful dates."

The conflict played out across her face, but whatever bothered her must have been pretty awful, because eventually she snatched the salt and limes off the bar, turned on her heel, and marched to the back staircase without another word. Carter took two of the shot glasses and the bottle of tequila, nodding to the bar manager as he followed Ruby. The manager sighed, "Thanks," and went about trying to get the clientele back.

Carter tried to put how good Ruby smelled out of his head. She was Natalia's best friend and the alpha of the BloodMoon pack, and pretty well off-limits. But his lion grumbled and growled as he found her pacing in the large living room upstairs, arms folded tightly to her chest and the expensive high-heeled boots she wore clicking across the floor. The lion liked the idea of a wolf alpha to curl up with at night. Carter set down the tequila and poured her another shot. She threw it back without a word, then leveled a look at him that nearly stopped his heart. "So you're dating now?"

He took his own drink and eased onto the couch after folding his jacket across the back of the chair. It had been a long damn day, bouncing between Natalia's restaurant and the Chase company headquarters to help Benedict. He put his feet up on the coffee table and yawned. "Logan's thing. He made me sign up with a matchmaker, so I've been on three blind dates in the last week. It's awful."

She managed a grimacing smile. "Really? I would have thought the matchmaker had pretty good instincts for that kind of thing."

"Oh, they all look good on paper." He rested his head on the back of the couch and stared up the ceiling fan, revolving in a lopsided circle. He glanced at her with a grin. "But on paper doesn't usually work out in real life, right?"

"Tell me about it." Ruby paused long enough for more tequila, swigging straight out of the bottle. She paced more, hands tapping patterns against her thighs, and Carter watched her walk. She wanted to talk, wanted to admit something, but she held herself back. After some time, she faced him, hands on her hips. "Don't tell anyone this or I will end you. Got it?"

He mimed zipping his lips and throwing away the key. God, she was beautiful – all fierce and fiery, pure energy and movement. Long dark hair falling over full breasts and a narrow waist, but with generous hips and a fantastic ass that just begged to be spanked. He tried to focus. And her threatening him was more than a little bit of a turn-on, if only because he wanted to show her how he felt about idle threats.

She took a deep breath, raking the hair back from her face, and started pacing again. "Miles Evershaw asked me to be his mate. Merge the packs, kick Rafe out, set up a power bloc against the rest of the shifters, and be mates. A marriage of convenience. A business deal."

Carter poured another shot and set out a lime wedge for her. "Sounds romantic. I'm surprised you didn't swoon."

She shot him a dirty look, but a hint of amusement gathered around her eyes. "Yeah."

"So what did you tell him?"

"No way in hell." She gave a frustrated growl and turned in a circle, searching the room for something he couldn't see. "He's an ass. And a control freak. He'd pretend up front that we would be equal, but I know him. There's only room for one alpha in his pack, and that's him. Everyone else is second. And I didn't bust my ass and fight half the wolves in this city to get where I'm at only to give it up for some dick."

Carter bit back a smile, even though he sympathized. "You shouldn't have to."

"No. And I'm not. Rafe and I made this pack. I'm not letting Miles fucking Evershaw run me off, or tell me there's no one else in the damn city who will date me."

Carter's dislike for Evershaw grew exponentially. The guy was a manipulative dick. He tried to intimidate Ruby into giving in, acting as if she would be alone forever. Carter raised a shot of tequila in salute. "I can refer you to my matchmaker. Then we can both have disappointing dates and bitch about them afterwards."

A smile definitely made an appearance. "Or not."

She took a shot, and then collapsed onto the couch next to him. She rubbed her forehead, fatigue suddenly evident in every line of her body. She smelled delicious, some kind of vanilla perfume clinging to her despite the liquor and the smoke from the bar. He wanted to pull her into his lap and cuddle her. Protect her.

Ruby took a deep breath and fixed him with a penetrating stare. "What's the matter with me, Carter?"

"Nothing. Absolutely nothing." His mouth was dry but the words came easily, and he wouldn't have looked away from her even if the entire pack came up the stairs to end his life. "You are fucking perfect."

"Then why is Miles Evershaw the only guy asking me out?"

He eased a little closer, dared to catch her knee and squeeze it. Even though what he really wanted was to grab her thighs and drag her closer so he could rip off her shirt. "Because you're successful and powerful, and you know what you want. Because you have high standards and you're not going to lower them because you know you're worth it."

Half of her mouth turned up. "That's what Nat would tell me. That's what women tell each other. Tell me from a man's perspective."

Carter's mind raced and his heart thumped, wanting to show her a man's perspective. Talking about it wasn't enough. Maybe the tequila made her vulnerable, maybe it was Natalia's impending wedding and all the bullshit that went along with it that had the normally unflappable Ruby thinking about why she hadn't found a mate. He leaned forward until they were nose to nose, but he kept his voice quiet so she had to ease forward even more, in order to hang on his every word. "Because you're in charge every minute of every day, men think you want that at home. In bed. And that makes them nervous."

"Makes them nervous." Her lips parted and she seemed very interested in his mouth. He heard her heart racing, could scent the hint of interest as her body reacted to his. "But not you, apparently."

"Because I know you don't really want to be in charge all the time." He smiled as she blinked and started to protest, and he touched the tips of his fingers to her lips, cutting her off. He leaned forward until she leaned back, giving way, and he braced his hands on either side of her shoulders, letting his knee depress the cushion between her thighs. He trapped her there, let her feel his weight, and dipped his head enough to nuzzle her hair. His voice dropped as he heard the thrum of her pulse. "I know you want someone else to be in charge when they take you to bed. You want someone to tell you what to do. Take away that burden of responsibility. Maybe tie you up. Teach you a lesson or two. And then let you saunter off to be alpha again, knowing you can't sit down because you got paddled for being a very bad girl."

Her breath escaped in something dangerously close to a moan, then Ruby blinked the dazed look away and braced her hands on his shoulders. "That's not at all what…"

"Don't lie to me." Carter grumbled a warning and rested his palm on her side, right against her rib cage. "I can hear your heart beating, Ruby."

She looked up at him, tense as a coiled spring, and her pupils dilated until her eyes looked completely black. "Maybe I'm about to throw you across this room."

Carter chuckled. But he sat back, unconcerned. Sometimes the game took longer than he wanted, but victory tasted better after anticipation. Before he got too far, Ruby's arms locked around his neck and she kissed him fiercely, demandingly. Carter waited only a moment before he kissed her back, fingers threading into her hair and tightening until he took control back. He pressed her back down on the couch and she moaned, writhing under him until the lion almost took over. He broke the kiss and retreated but kept her pinned, studying her expression as she panted, eyes wide.

He lowered his head and brushed his lips against hers before easing back. She started to follow him, ready for another kiss, but he tightened his hold on her hair and she inhaled sharply. Carter smiled, returned for another slow kiss. She tasted like tequila and lime and lust, a heady mix with threads of her own taste as well. Ruby bit at his lip, and Carter immediately withdrew. She arched, wanting more contact, but he kept his distance as he murmured, "Here's the thing, Ruby. I like being the one in charge, but I'm not looking for a fight. So whether or not we do this – that's up to you. We'll establish a few ground rules before this goes anywhere, though, and make sure we're on the same page."

"You're saying you won't fuck me unless you get to tie me up?"

Carter shook his head and tapped the end of her nose. "It's not about restraints. It's about acknowledging what you want – what you need. But no, you're not going to intimidate me into sex, and I'm not taking you to bed tonight regardless."

Her full breasts pressed against his chest and Carter immediately regretted his decision. Ruby knew it, could feel his arousal, and undulated her hips against his in a deliberate motion that nearly finished him. Her voice went husky and low. "You sure about that, Carter?"

"Yes." He pushed up and got off the couch, adjusting his clothes as he poured another shot of tequila. He downed it, then picked up his jacket from the back of the chair. A bit of mindful breathing helped resolve the problem in his pants, and he faced her with a clear mind. "So here's the deal. I like you. A lot. And I think we would have an unbelievable amount of fun together."

“That might not be enough,” she said, still sprawled across the couch. She looked ready to be thrown over his shoulder and carried away. Carter sucked in a breath and focused on his mantra. Had to stay centered. Control was important. Ruby cleared her throat and looked away, a flush rising in her cheeks. “Regardless of what I may… enjoy in bed, I can’t have a weak mate. I can’t have people think that…”

“So a lion would be a weak mate?” She flushed, about to rephrase, but he just held up his hand to cut her off. “What do you care what people think? You’re the alpha. You can do what you want, right?”

“It’s not that easy.” She looked regretful, maybe sad. “It’s never that easy.”

“It could be.” He shrugged, wondering if he needed to call Edgar for a ride before heading back to the house. The security chief worked late in the city, and after Carter killed half a bottle of tequila, driving might not be the best idea. And he sure as shit couldn’t stay in the same house as Ruby – his resolve wouldn’t last the entire night. “It’s your choice, Ruby. If you want to talk more, let me know.”

He forced himself to walk away despite the sound she made, as if she wanted to have the last word. He didn’t look back.

chapter 3

The only reason I bothered to drag myself out of bed the next morning was because I had to meet Natalia for brunch. And she always knew the best places to eat. If she recommended brunch at a dodgy as hell hole-in-the-wall, chances were it was transcendent and about to be the biggest thing in the city. So I hauled myself up, got dressed, and went to meet her across the city.

I tried to put Carter's words out of my head as I revved my motorcycle. When he said I wanted someone to take over in the bedroom, part of me immediately denied it. Of course I didn't want some guy to tell me what to do, tie me up, take over. Of course not. But a shiver of excitement ran through me at his words, and the mental image of me handcuffed to the headboard and him crawling over the bed toward me…I shook it off and concentrated on the bike.

But that fire in his eyes stayed with me. I'd never seen Carter like that before. He was always the quiet brother, shy and sweet, helping his brothers out with whatever needed to be done. He played guitar in the bar sometimes when someone had a birthday party, and he never bumped chests or got into fights with any of the pack. He was just…Carter. But the way he'd moved over me, trapped me, kissed me… I swallowed hard. Holy shit. I'd never been kissed like that.

I parked the bike and looked around as I took off my helmet. Natalia sure knew how to pick 'em – the neighborhood looked seriously dicey, just a couple of blocks from where the bears set up their MMA gym. I'd been meaning to check out what Kaiser and the guys were doing, because several of my pack wanted to train there. Maybe I could pop by after brunch, drag Natalia over with me so they would behave themselves. I took my helmet inside with me, not liking the looks of some of the younger kids loitering across the street.

She sat in the back, concentrating on a menu, but got up when I walked in. She hugged me and gave up her seat, so I could have my back to a wall and still see the door. Nat looked a little pale, dark circles under her eyes, and I frowned as I eased into my chair. "What's wrong? You look like hell."

"Thanks, Ruby." She rolled her eyes but didn't go on, and I knew something really was up.

When the server approached, she ordered ginger ale and some sort of chicken and puff pastry dish; I shrugged and got the same thing. If it turned out to be terrible, there was at least one dirty water hotdog cart between this place and the gym. I folded my hands on the table and watched her. "What's up, Nat?"

Her lips pursed and my heart sank. Oh Lord. She and Logan were breaking up, and the lions were about to go ape-shit on the city. The lion alpha would lose his fucking mind if he lost Natalia. I'd known both of them separately for a long time, and while I had every confidence Natalia would be fine, Logan might never recover. I started calculating how much damage control the Council would have to do, and whether Edgar could be relied on to support us in containing his brother, but Nat kept talking.

"You know we're having a party at the end of next week, right? The one to celebrate Logan's birthday?"

"Sure," I said, cautious.

"It's going to be our wedding."

I snorted coffee through my nose, and choked. She dodged out of the way, making a face, and handed me a stack of tissue-thin napkins from the dispenser. I coughed and hacked to get the burning liquid out of my lungs, but at least it gave me an excuse for the tears stinging my eyes. "Your what?"

"Our wedding. We didn't want to wait."

"Christ," I muttered, wiping at my nose and eyes. "Why not? There's no rush, really…" and I cut off, because her hand rested on her stomach and my heart jumped to my throat. It couldn't be.

She looked the slightest bit uncertain. "I'm pregnant. And I don't want to be a fat bride. We thought I'd still be able to fit into my dress in two weeks, but much past that and I'll start testing the tensile strength of the fabric."

"Holy shit." I coughed more, pounding on my chest, and waved away the concerned waiter. I tried to buy time to think and breathe with a long sip of water, but it didn't help. I still didn't know what to say. "Congratulations?"

"Thank you." She flushed, looking away. "I'm happy about it. We're happy about it. Surprised, but really, really happy. I wasn't sure how you would…"

"Jesus, Nat, of course I'm happy for you." I lurched up and dragged her into a hug, squeezing her tightly. "How could you doubt for a second that I would be anything but over the moon for you?"

She hugged me back, sounding a bit wobbly herself. "Well, I know you've been wanting…"

"What I want doesn't take away from what you have." I held her at arm's length and scowled at her, wanting her to believe me all the way to her bones. "You fat cow. Of *course* I'm happy for you, and of course I'll be the kid's godmother, and of course I'll spoil the hell out of it. Always. Don't ever think for a second that I'm jealous of your happiness."

Even if I was, a little. More than a little.

"I know it's stupid," she said. Natalia sank back into her chair and patted her cheeks with a napkin. "It's a surprise that the party is the wedding, though so don't tell anyone. You'll still be my maid of honor?"

"Absolutely." I took a deep breath and wondered if I would have to find a date for the party now as well. Rafe would be out of town, and while I didn't mind going by myself since so many friends would be there, it sure as hell would be nice to have someone to go home with. "What can I do to help?"

"Not much, for now." She smiled and leaned back as the waiter brought our food, and waited until he'd retreated to go on. "Logan's so paranoid about me and the baby that he practically won't let us out of the house. I have three different party planners at my beck and call, so anything I say out-loud pretty much occurs whether I really wanted it to or not."

I shook my head, poking the odd dish with my fork. "What the hell is this?"

"It's amazing. Based on a Moroccan dish, I forget the name. Filo dough, shredded chicken, spices, powdered sugar... It's amazing. Seriously. Just trust me — try it." She dug in, powdered sugar flying up in a cloud, and I watched with raised eyebrows, impressed. Nat, being a professional chef, always liked to eat, but being pregnant must have flipped a switch.

So I tasted some of the pastry and chicken, and grudgingly had to admit it melted in my mouth like a little piece of heaven. She grinned, on the verge of saying she told me so, but her phone rang and she rolled her eyes instead. "Logan, checking in. Just a sec."

As she told her soon-to-be-husband to mind his business and leave her alone, I sat back and looked around the empty restaurant. Maybe Nat would have an opinion on the thing with Carter. She lived with the kid, after all. After she hung up, my best friend pushed back her plate with a groan. "I'll have to take the rest of it home. Now what's up with you, Ruby? You're not yourself."

"It's been a weird week." I pushed some crust across the plate, for some reason reticent to share too much. Natalia was still fully human, and dragging her into shifter politics more than Logan already did wasn't something I wanted to be responsible for. She was vulnerable the way only a human could be, and now she carried Logan's child. Allowing her to be hurt, or even scared, would be my death sentence.

When I paused too long, she kicked my leg under the table and fixed me with a familiar scowl. "Look, you. Weird shit is happening to both of us, and before this gets too out of hand and I start talking about breast milk and stretch marks and not being able to hold my pee, you're going to tell me what the hell is going on in your life."

And that was why I loved that girl. I'd been so glad when she met Logan and finally learned about shifters, because it had always been a huge secret between us. I'd hated the lies. So I took a deep breath and gave her my own scowl. "Fine, but you can't tell anyone. Not Logan, not Edgar, not Rafe, not Eloise — *no one*. On penalty of me never speaking to you again and tripping you as you walk down the aisle. Got it?"

"Idle threats, idle threats. But go on." She touched her stomach again, absently, as if she could tell something grew there.

I pressed the heels of my hands to my eyes, wishing I'd had time for more coffee or at least less time for tequila the night before. "Last night, Miles Evershaw propositioned me."

She snorted a laugh, then picked up her phone. "So you murdered him? Do I need to call Edgar to go clean up the bodies?"

"No, of course not. He just…it's a business proposition for him. He's got zero emotion. He said no other man in the city would ask me out, so I might as well give up and mate with him." It hurt to admit in the daylight, when the anger of the first telling no longer sustained me. I wanted to be only angry about it, but his words cut more deeply than I could admit. It hurt. Maybe in part because I feared he was right.

"Well, that's total bullshit." Natalia picked at her food, though she gave me a jaundiced look. "Are you tempted?"

"Offended, more like." My fingers drummed on the table as I stared past her shoulder to the door as another couple of diners arrived. "But then I started thinking, what if he's right? What if my only chance to be mated and have kids is with him? He's such an asshole."

"Okay, heifer." She leaned forward and smacked the table near my hand, making me jump. "You look at me and hear every fucking word I say. He is not right. You will find someone amazing to be with, you will have amazing, beautiful babies. You will not shack up with Miles Evershaw and have little half-asshole babies. I won't allow it."

"Easy for you to say. You're not an alpha. A wolf would have to be stone crazy to ask me out. It would be an almost automatic challenge to Rafe, and then…I wouldn't be able to relax. What if he asked me out just to get me vulnerable in order to challenge me and then fight, so he could take over the pack? How can I trust any wolf?"

"Does he have to be a wolf?" Natalia drained her ginger ale and gestured for the waiter to bring more. "Why not one of the bears? Or Edgar? He seems a bit gruff for you, but at least if you're dating someone who isn't a wolf, you don't have to worry about them taking over your pack. I mean, Rafe would be cool with both of you still being alphas, even if you mated a non-wolf, right?"

"Of course, he's my brother. He doesn't mind the physical work of running the pack, he just wants me to do the business end. And keep the women in line. He hates the drama."

"Bitches be crazy," Nat said thoughtfully, then asked the waiter to see the dessert menu. That was one of the best things about Nat – she enjoyed food and eating, and she always ordered dessert. Even if she was a bit nuts most of the time.

I gathered my courage to tell her the rest of it, my palms a little sweaty as I gripped the edge of the table. "So after I left Evershaw's office, I went to the bar. And Carter was there."

"Carter? I wonder where he'd got to. He looked a bit rough this morning at yoga."

I leaned my elbows on the table and raised my eyebrows. "Yoga?"

"Yeah, he leads yoga and mindful breathing for the family in the mornings now. It really helps Sophia and Atticus, they've both got control issues to work on, and apparently the meditation really helps. I join in because I like the stretching. But Carter looked like death warmed over." She smiled. "So that was your fault?"

"Partially." I flushed but didn't know why, looking away. "I took the edge off with some tequila and he helped. And then he said…well, he said he liked me. And wanted to ask me out, but would leave it up to me."

Her eyebrows climbed to her hairline as she sat back, mouth ajar.

"Exactly," I said, putting my face in my hands. "It's Carter. *Carter.*"

"What did you say?" she managed to splutter.

"Nothing. I didn't have time. He said it, said it was up to me, and then he left." I held my hands up, still a little stunned. I didn't need to tell her the part about him wanting to tie me up. That might make her head explode, to think sweet Carter was a whips and chains kind of guy in the bedroom.

"Carter?" Nat shook her head but ordered some kind of weird yogurt and fruit dessert before turning her attention back to me. "I didn't think you were his type. I mean, I pictured him with a librarian. Or a kindergarten teacher. Someone sweet and quiet and…not you. Not at all you."

I laughed. "Thanks?"

"You know what I mean. You're an alpha. You get what you want. I just don't see how he would…compete with that." She frowned in thought, folding and refolding a napkin. "But I guess he wouldn't need to, would he? As long as he made you happy, it wouldn't really matter what the rest of the world thought. It wouldn't matter whether he could control the pack, because that would never be an issue. Right?"

"Well..." I played with my fork, a muscle in my jaw jumping. "I don't know how to say this, Nat, so don't take it wrong. I don't know if he gives the right impression for me. I'm a tough chick, I'm an alpha, I lead the strongest pack in this city. I need a guy who's strong enough, impressive enough to match that. You know? And Carter's…nice. He's a nice guy. He's sweet. He doesn't get in anyone's face."

"He would in a second if he thought that someone was bothering me, or Eloise, or Sophia, or you. When Eloise faced down the hyenas and one of them threatened her, Carter was the one who killed the hyena queen. He changed the fastest, he fought through the extra hyenas, he didn't hesitate to protect her – and he barely knew her. Just because he's quiet and laid back doesn't mean he can't turn on the crazy when needed."

I rubbed my forehead. "I don't know."

"Give him a chance." She lit up as the waiter arrived, putting the parfait dish and mess of yogurt and fruit and rosewater syrup in the middle of the table to share. "Go on a date with him, at least. He's going to this matchmaker, and so far none of the dates have gone very well."

"Don't tell anyone, okay? Seriously. I can't take the teasing."

"Who would tease?" Natalia made a significant dent in the dessert before pointing the spoon at me. "They might tease him, but I'm guessing if anyone said a cross word to you, Carter would make them disappear. He's good at that. And he's a fantastic businessman. Really, since he's been managing my restaurant, we've tripled our profit. I don't know how he does it. We weren't making that much money even when we were a criminal front."

I managed a smile, and even tasted some of the weird ass dessert. "I'll think about it. Now. For the wedding in two weeks, what do we need to get done?"

She sighed and started talking about dress fittings for both of us. I listened to most of it, but thoughts of Carter distracted me. There was a lot to lose if things didn't go well, but then again, he was the first non-asshole who sort of asked me out in at least a year. And Nat supported it. I held my breath and forced myself to concentrate on the wedding planning details. I had a week to give Evershaw an answer, so that meant a week to try Carter on without committing. I always worked better with a deadline.

chapter 4

The bears' gym stayed open at all hours, even if the bears always looked like they'd just woken up from a nap. Carter knew the code to the front door and let himself in right after leaving the mansion. He always did yoga at dawn, but lately the number of participants increased so much he couldn't focus on his own relaxation. Kaiser and the bears were kind enough to trade some of his business planning for unfettered access to their workout space.

He went into the back room, recently converted into a makeshift locker room, and changed into workout gear. He had an hour, maybe two, before meeting Logan at the company headquarters. He hadn't slept well at all, between the tequila and images of Ruby. Her scent clung to his clothes, taunted him, drove him crazy with half-waking dreams until his lion seethed and grumbled about chasing after her.

Carter wrapped his hands as he walked back into the main gym. Two of the bears, Owen and Axel, lumbered in from the backyard and nodded to him. Owen looked half-asleep as he offered to hold a heavy bag for Carter, and soon enough Carter lost himself in the easy rhythm of punches and body kicks against the bag.

And yet, still Ruby distracted him. Funny how he'd known her for so long and yet the simmering interest hadn't boiled over into anything physical. He'd always found her attractive, his lion always scented her with interest, but she was never someone who seemed open to romance. Owen, a shock of black hair falling across his forehead, grunted as Carter slammed his knee into the bag in frustration, and the bear backed up a few steps to recover.

As Carter ducked back and lifted his guard again before the next assault on the bag, a bell rang. Owen blinked and yawned, then shuffled toward the door. "Visitors. You expecting anyone, Axel?"

The polar bear, whipping the speed bag so fast his fists blurred, merely grunted. "No."

Carter turned, wiping the sweat from his face, and froze. Ruby and Natalia stood outside the giant glass-front doors. He steeled his nerves as Natalia bulled through the door as soon as Owen opened it, Ruby close on her heels. Owen let them in, looking a bit taken aback, and managed to say, "Kaiser's in his pool, I'll go get him," before heading toward the back door.

"Carter?" Natalia noticed him but slanted a sideways look at the Viking polar bear growling and smacking the bag around before she approached the heavy bags. "What are you doing here?"

"Working out." He didn't look at Ruby, not knowing how she would react after the way he'd left the night before, and wiped his face with the front of his t-shirt. "What are you guys doing over here?"

"Oh, Ruby and I had brunch nearby." Nat eyed him askance, and Carter knew immediately Ruby told her something. He fought to keep his equilibrium and remain aloof and unruffled, knowing Ruby would look for how he reacted under pressure. Natalia wrinkled her nose as she looked around. "She wanted to talk to Kaiser about the gym. I thought I'd tag along. I did not realize it would smell so… ripe."

Carter nodded, then rubbed his jaw as burly Kaiser lumbered in from outside, wearing only a towel and rubbing his hair with another. Even the alpha bear, a half-polar half-grizzly grolar bear, looked like he'd been caught dozing. Kaiser smiled at the women and gently pressed their fingers with his, as if he feared bruising them by a handshake alone. "What can I do for you?"

Ruby shoved her hands in the pockets of her tight jeans, surveying the gym, and studied Kaiser with a critical eye. "Benedict said you started some MMA training and other stuff for shifters. Some of my pack are interested in participating. I want to make sure they're not going to be exploited or committed to rank fights if they cross someone here."

Kaiser finished rubbing his short hair and tossed the towel across his shoulder. It didn't cover much of his massive pecs or traps. "Everyone who joins signs a contract. Benedict agreed to draw it up for me so it's legally binding, and the Council will ratify that it will absolve the signatories from any rank implications of fighting in this gym."

She mulled it over, and her gaze strayed to Carter. She flushed when she realized she was staring at him, and snapped her attention back to Kaiser. "Okay. If the Council ratifies it, BloodMoon would be happy to utilize your facilities. Do you give group discounts?"

"You'll have to discuss that with my business manager," the bear said, and nodded at Carter. Ruby's flush climbed a little higher, and Carter bit back his glee. Kaiser, apparently oblivious, turned and wandered toward his office. "I'll show you the price breakdown. I'm sure we can work something out, O'Shea."

"I'm sure," she said under her breath, and Carter pinched the bridge of his nose so he wouldn't watch her ass as she stormed after him. Jeans like hers should be illegal.

He hesitated, about to follow, then jumped as Natalia pinched his side. "What the hell, Nat?"

The chef gave him an arch look. "What are your intentions toward my friend?"

Carter laughed, then caught her arm and drew her away from the office, so hopefully Ruby's supernatural hearing wouldn't pick up on what they said. "The ball is in her court, Nat. Entirely."

"She's my dearest friend," Natalia said, lowering her voice as she poked him in the chest. Even being half a foot shorter than him and easily half his weight, she still managed to make him step back. "And she is amazing, Carter. She deserves much better."

"I know." He caught Nat's shoulders and held her back a little to avoid any more bruises. She had sharp fingers. "And I'm offended that you think I wouldn't treat her well."

"That's not what I said." Natalia rubbed her stomach, frowning over his shoulder at where Ruby played hardball with Kaiser. "It's just…we've both got some hard edges, Ruby and I. We're used to keeping people away. And I want her to be happy."

"Of course." Carter grumbled and pulled Natalia into a sweaty hug, making sure her face ended up near his armpit just because, and she spluttered and shouted as she tried to get away.

He laughed even with the death-glares from Natalia as the chef backed up and made a face at the sweat and damp. Carter gave her a winning smile, knowing perfectly well Natalia wouldn't stay mad at him. "It's her call, Nat, and she's a big girl. She can make her own decisions."

"She does. Believe me, she does." Natalia took a breath and checked her phone as it rang. "But she has to think of Rafe and her pack and everything, and sometimes…well, hell. Every single time, she puts their welfare and what they want ahead of what she needs. What she deserves. So don't be a jerk. Please."

"I'm not a jerk," he said under his breath, then pointed at the phone. "Answer it. Logan will just keep calling. And calling. And calling..."

"I know." She scowled at the phone, then held it up to her ear. "*What?*" She paced as she talked, ignoring the two other bears that wandered into the gym.

Carter nodded to them, about to ask if one wanted to spar, but stopped as Owen muttered, "Shit," and the doorbell rang again.

Miles Evershaw and half a dozen of his best fighters waited outside. Owen lackadaisically headed to the door, glancing back at the office where Kaiser and Ruby continued an intense conversation. Axel, the Viking polar bear, straightened from his abuse of the speed bag and scowled at the door. "Fucking wolves."

Carter crossed his arms over his chest and stared at the door. He didn't normally want to punch Miles Evershaw right in the face, but after hearing what he told Ruby, that seemed like the best course of action. The alpha of the SilverLine pack brushed past Owen with barely a nod, and scanned the room for threats or challengers as he strode in, the pack on his heels. He noted Carter's presence with a slight dip of his chin, but he paused and scented the air. His gaze went first to Natalia, still on the phone with Logan, and then to the office where Ruby argued. A smile touched Evershaw's face and Carter wanted to hit him even more.

Instead, Carter strode forward to shake the wolf's hand. "Evershaw. What brings you here?"

"Business with the bear," Evershaw said, and jerked his chin at the back office. Kaiser noted their presence and shuffled toward the main area, and Ruby looked like she wanted to flee. Carter maneuvered himself so he stood between the alpha and Ruby. Just in case.

Kaiser frowned as he lumbered over and shook Evershaw's hand. "Busy this morning. No one calls ahead anymore."

"I didn't think you were open yet," Evershaw said. His gaze remained on Ruby as she sauntered over, unwilling to let two other alphas talk without being part of the conversation. The SilverLine alpha took a wider stance, arms folded over his chest, and raised his eyebrows. "But apparently you're letting all kinds of people in today."

Ruby opened her mouth to retort, but Kaiser cut her off with a warning grumble. "This is neutral territory, Evershaw. And it's still my den, so I let in whoever the fuck I want. You got a problem with that?"

The wolf didn't blink. "No problem with you, Kaiser. Just curious about why BloodMoon was so eager to get over here with the lions in tow."

"The lion was here first," Carter said, bristling. Evershaw couldn't speak without a challenge in his voice. "So step back."

Miles's face lost all expression and his shoulders grew as he reacted to the challenge. His pack arrayed out behind him, each one eying Carter, and Kaiser, and Ruby. Ready to fight. Carter debated unwrapping his hands before the brawl started, if only so he could cause more damage, and loosened the grips as he watched Evershaw. He wished at least Atticus was with him, but Kaiser and his bears wouldn't let things get out of hand. Still, a lion could hold off a wolf pack. He'd done it before.

Ruby growled, her eyes flashing gold as she edged around Kaiser and elbowed Carter in the ribs. "Cut it out, Evershaw, no one's going to…"

"Not now, Ruby." Evershaw dropped his chin as he eyed Carter and flexed his fists. "I'll deal with you later."

She bared her teeth, lurching forward as Kaiser blocked her from getting too close to the other alpha. A deafening growl built in the bear's chest. "No blood will be spilled here unless I'm the one spilling it."

Carter braced himself to take on the wolf pack, hoping the bears would come in on his side. The tension simmered as he stared Evershaw down, and the lion wanted to defend Ruby. He might have leapt at the SilverLine alpha just to break the silence, except Natalia patted him on the back and marched to stand in front of Evershaw.

Natalia squinted at him, her phone still in her hand as she studied the unblinking alpha. "So you're the asshole everyone's talking about."

Kaiser snorted and Evershaw blinked, jostled out of the challenge with Carter, and stared down at her. "I beg your pardon."

The human tapped her chin as she studied him. "You don't *look* like an asshole. I mean, you helped Eloise out when she needed it, right? So what's with the posturing?"

Evershaw looked from her to Ruby, then Carter, then back to Natalia. "Who are you?"

"Natalia," Carter said, before she could speak, and he gripped her elbow to tug her out of the circle of bristling shifters. "Logan's mate."

"Logan's mate," Evershaw repeated. He studied her critically, then shook his head. "You're human. I don't see the point."

Nat scowled as Carter dragged her out of harm's way, and she muttered, "Now I get it. He's an *asshole*."

Carter parked her near Owen, with a few words for the bear. "If anyone starts fighting, take her somewhere safe. If she gets so much as a scratch, Logan will kill everyone in at least a three block radius."

Just as he returned to face the group, Evershaw gave Ruby a once-over and raised his eyebrow. "Neutral territory, O'Shea. You got something you want to tell me?"

Before she could respond, Carter's lion growled – loud and angry enough even Kaiser looked up. A snarl wanted to follow but he choked it back when he saw Ruby's face and her struggle to remain in control. He didn't want to fan the flames, but every atom in his body wanted to kill Miles Evershaw for daring to proposition her. For daring to treat her like a business deal.

chapter 5

Despite seeing a sweaty Carter as soon as we walked into the gym, everything was going fine as I negotiated with Kaiser for a group rate. I'd send every one of my pack to him for training. We needed better fighters, more methodical and tactically proficient fighters. As it was, BloodMoon tended to brawl, or at least go for the melee. And that wasn't how you expanded to become the only pack in the city. And the state.

Evershaw thought he was the only wolf with ambitions, but I'd had my eyes on a bigger prize far longer than he had.

And as if my thoughts summoned him, Evershaw and a handful of his misfit toys showed up at the gym to challenge Kaiser, and me, and Carter. It wasn't an accident. Nothing happened to Miles Evershaw accidentally. I braced for a hell of a confrontation as Carter marched Natalia across the room and put her some place safe, and waited for the SilverLine alpha to make his move. Instead, he just watched me. Said something about me telling him something in the tone he always used: condescending asshole.

But Carter surprised me. The moment Evershaw eyed me, surveying me like he owned me, the lion reacted. He bristled, and something close to a roar rumbled through his chest. My cheeks heated as Kaiser raised his eyebrows and studied Carter, trying to figure out what pissed off the lion. I really didn't want him to find out. I folded my arms over my chest and stood my ground. I couldn't give an inch, otherwise I'd never gain it back. "I've got nothing to say to you, Evershaw."

Before he could respond, Kaiser elbowed between us and planted a hand on the other alpha's chest, while pointing his other massive mitt in my direction. "Until we have the agreement ratified by the Council, BloodMoon and SilverLine will have to schedule their time separately. I will not tolerate this stupidity in my gym. You can growl all you want about it, but I've never heard of a wolf taking on a grizzly *or* a polar bear, and you've got both of them right here. So which one of you wants to test me?"

I felt, suddenly, like my mother had scolded me for fighting with Rafe. At least Kaiser didn't use my middle name. I refused to speak first, staring Evershaw down. His teeth flashed white as he made an angry noise, then fixed Kaiser with a dark look. "We'll be back at two."

"Fine." Kaiser folded his arms over his chest and nodded at the door. "See yourselves out. And next time, leave your backup dancers outside, Evershaw."

Evershaw looked on the verge of speaking once more, particularly as he looked at me, then turned on his heel and strode out. His pack followed, though more than one turned back to look at me. Or maybe at Kaiser, who was still damn impressive, and still wearing only a towel. Once the door shut behind them and they disappeared around the corner, I exhaled.

The bear studied me for a long moment, then canted his head at the office. "We'll finish up with our agreement. And Carter?" He waited until the lion looked at him to point at the corner. "Please retrieve your human before she damages Owen."

I looked back in time to see Natalia pinching Owen's side and lecturing him about something, no doubt that he'd been eating too much jam and cake. Or that he hadn't been eating *enough* jam and cake. Carter sighed and shook his head as he moved in that direction, rubbing his shoulder. "I swear, I can't take her anywhere."

As much as I wanted to see what Nat did when Carter tried to redirect her, I followed Kaiser to the office and took my seat in front of the desk. Kaiser sat behind the battered wooden contraption, held together with rubber bands and duct tape, and leaned his elbows on a few stacks of paper as he watched me. "What was all that about?"

"Evershaw is a —"

"I meant Carter." The bear remained remarkably expressionless. "Is there going to be an issue if you're here fighting and he sees someone take a swing at you?"

"No idea what you're talking about." I prayed the warmth in my cheeks wasn't visible.

Kaiser fixed me with a look. "Don't bullshit me, O'Shea. I know what I heard."

"There's nothing going on."

He didn't believe me. His nose wrinkled and he rubbed his jaw. "Then why does Evershaw have his knickers in a twist?"

"Because he's an asshole?" When the bear opened his mouth again, I leaned forward and tapped the contract we'd been negotiating. "Do you want to gossip about our mutual acquaintances, or do you want to finish this up?"

His head tilted, and Kaiser's dark eyes narrowed. I refused to speak or look away, even though my pulse pounded in my throat. I didn't want to challenge the bear; Kaiser had always been nice to me, to my pack, and I didn't want to burn that bridge. Plus a wolf pack would be hard-pressed to subdue a bear his size, and my pack would take at least thirty minutes to get there. So a lone wolf had to be a smart wolf.

Kaiser exhaled loudly. He leaned forward as well, until we were nearly nose-to-nose, and his voice huffed into the silence. "We'll finish this up, O'Shea, but take some advice, free of charge. Keep an eye on both those men. I don't know who's more dangerous for you."

"Carter would never hurt me," I said under my breath, wanting to scoot my chair back so I could breathe. "And Evershaw isn't that stupid."

"You're wrong on both counts," he said, impassive. He picked up the agreement and tossed it across the desk. "Regardless, you'll pay this amount monthly for unlimited access. There will be a unique code on the door for your pack to use. If I find out they've given the code to anyone, the contract is terminated and you're not welcome back. Understood?"

"That won't be a problem." I pushed aside unease from what he'd said. Kaiser couldn't really think that Carter would hurt me. Or that Evershaw would try something really underhanded. Evershaw generally kept his ass-hole-ness upfront and in your face. I studied the sheet and tried not to flinch. That amount of money...the bar would definitely have to stay open every night to try to pay the tab. But I had to invest in the pack if we wanted to take over the city. So I took a deep breath and held out my hand. "It's a deal."

He shook my hand with his enormous grip and I could have sworn my bones creaked. He nodded, said, "Deal," and rose from behind the desk. His towel started to slip and I turned on my heel, cheeks red. I could maintain my composure facing his well-furred chest and eight-pack abs, but I wasn't stone.

Out in the gym, Carter argued quietly with Natalia. She scowled when she saw me, giving me a half-hug before heading for the door. "Carter tattled on me to Logan, so I've gotta get home before the ole boy loses his head. You'll be okay?" She shot a dark look at the lion.

"We've got it sorted." I waved her off. "I'll call you later."

She strode off, muttering into her phone, and I faced Carter. He shook his head, watching as she left, and took a deep breath. "For a second there, I thought Logan might kill me."

I snorted, fighting a smile. "What are you doing here, anyway?"

"Working out." He gestured at his gym clothes and the rapidly drying t-shirt. "I keep the books for Kaiser, so he lets me work out here for free."

"You keep the books? Like, the finances?"

"Yeah." Carter's smile grew, a little amused as he studied me. "I've got an MBA, I'm qualified."

"Shut up." I put my hands on my hips as I stared at him. "You have an MBA?"

Carter laughed, shaking his head as he looked at the ground, then ran a hand through his hair. "Apparently there's a lot you don't know about me."

"Well…"

"So let's change that." Carter glanced over his shoulder at where Kaiser spoke with Owen near the office, his towel once more secure, then smiled at me. "Have dinner with me."

"I can't." A surge of adrenaline made my hands shake. I couldn't. If anyone saw us out together, they would assume we were dating and then everything would get way too complicated.

"That was fast." He laughed and started unwrapping his hands. "Call it a business meeting. Bring the records for the bar and I'll take a look at them."

"A business meeting." My stomach wobbled, and I clenched my hands together behind my back. It was tempting, especially when he smiled at me and got that mischievous twinkle in his eyes. "I don't know if…"

"Tonight." He glanced at his phone, then frowned. "Seven o'clock. You want me to pick you up, or will you meet me there?"

"I…" My thoughts couldn't keep up with his plans, and I struggled to form a coherent response. "I'll meet you. Where?"

"Haven't decided yet." He glanced at me, eyebrow raised, and the smile grew. "I'll call you in a bit."

He headed for what I assumed was the locker room and I stared after him, still a little uncertain about how I agreed to go on a date with him. Shaking my head, I caught Kaiser watching me from the doorway of his office, arms crossed. I started to tell him it wasn't what it looked like, but the words died in my throat. It was exactly what it looked like.

So instead, I held up a hand to cut off whatever he hadn't said, and headed for the door. "I'll cut you the check tomorrow, Kaiser."

At least the air outside cooled the burn from my cheeks, and my helmet hid the rest as I stalked to the motorcycle at the curb. Every time my phone pinged with a new message, a frisson of excitement ran through me and I both hoped for and dreaded the arrival of Carter's text.

By the time I got back to the bar, I could hardly concentrate enough not to lay the bike down in a heap, and I strode through the back without acknowledging anyone. Rafe sat in the office, frowning at spreadsheets full of information. I paused in the doorway. “Hey. You busy?”

“Nah.” He rubbed his forehead as he tossed the paper aside and leaned back in his chair. “You were up early.”

He always knew when something bothered me, part of the price and gift of being twins. I eased into the office and kicked the door closed behind me. “Met Nat for brunch. We went to Kaiser’s gym and I got the price for a monthly pack membership. We’ll need to sell a shitload of beer.”

He snorted and put his feet up on the desk, staring up at the ceiling with a sigh. “Shit, Bee. I don’t know if the bar is the way to do that. We might need to branch out.”

“I’ve got a plan for that.” Lying to Rafe was always difficult, if not impossible. He could read me like a book. “I’m meeting Carter tonight to go over the books, see where we might be able to improve things. Maybe branch out.”

“Carter?” Rafe frowned, his dark eyebrows more like fuzzy caterpillars. “He handles Nat’s restaurant, so maybe he’ll have something useful to say. You want me to come?”

“If you want.” I shrugged, even though my heart sped up to think of bringing Rafe on my date with Carter. That wouldn’t go over well. “But who’d cover the bar?”

My brother’s head tilted as he studied me. “You go. Just let me know what he says. And tell me what’s really bothering you, because I know something’s up.”

My fingers drummed on the arm of my chair, and I put my boots up next to Rafe’s on the corner of the desk. I studied the boots, not him, as I went on. “Met with Evershaw last night.”

Rafe's eyes narrowed. "You didn't say anything."

"He wanted to talk to me alone." I held up my hands. "I just wanted to hear what he had to say. And it's a good thing you weren't there, because you might have killed him. He wants to combine our packs, align against the rest of the shifters, and take me as his mate."

I knew him well enough to see the rage in his eyes and the bulging vein in his temple, despite that Rafe looked only moderately interested in what I said. He read between the lines well enough to know there wouldn't be room for him in Evershaw's pack. He swallowed before he spoke. "I see."

"I told him no way." I shoved to my feet and tried to pace in the cramped office, but only made it three steps before I had to about-face. "Obviously. But he's pushing for only one wolf pack in the city. Which is why we have to get our shit together. We can't count on the lions, or the bears, or anyone else. Just us. Just pack."

Rafe stared at something only he could see, and after a long silence, he looked at me. "Were you tempted?"

"By Evershaw?" I snorted, giving up on the pacing to just stand there. "Don't be ridiculous. Of course not."

"Bec," he said, and leaned his elbows on the desk. "Look. We might have to consider breaking up the pack, or one of us splitting off. There aren't a whole lot of wolves that would mate with you but let me stick around as alpha. And there aren't a whole lot of wolves that would mate with me but let you stick around as alpha. We've got a unique set-up, and it's worked for us, but I don't know if it's sustainable long-term. You know?"

Swallowing grew difficult. "You're fucking kidding me. You want me to go with Evershaw?"

"That's not what I said." Rafe sighed, and rubbed his face. "But come on, Bee. I know you want kids. I want kids. That's not going to be easy the way things are now. How long do we wait?"

We looked at each other in silence for way too long. My heartbeat echoed in my ears and I felt like I was drowning. "We worked too hard for this, Rafe. Gave up too much to just walk away."

He eased to his feet. "I'm not walking away. Just… —think about how this can work for us, with families, going forward."

I wanted to hit him. Instead, I walked out of the office and headed for the basement to start hauling kegs and crates up for the night.

chapter 6

Even as he arrived at the upscale Italian restaurant exactly at seven, Carter wasn't entirely certain Ruby would show up. When he'd called with the name and address of the restaurant, after he confirmed he could actually get a reservation, she sounded distracted and upset. Breathing hard, like she'd been exercising or crying. So he mentally prepared to be stood up, and figured he'd give her thirty minutes before he called Edgar to join him instead.

But at five past seven, the maître d' escorted her around the dance floor and toward the table, and Carter stood to pull out her chair. She looked fucking amazing. She wore a simple black dress, tight in all the right places before it flared out, with a crimson sash and a strand of pearls. The colorful tattoos on her arms and back only added to the allure. She'd pulled her hair back in a high ponytail, exposing the long column of her neck, and all he could think about was nibbling on the white flesh. Marking her. Leaving hickies and bites until everyone knew she was claimed.

She raised her eyebrows as she paused by the chair he'd pulled out. "Well?"

"Well what?"

"Do I pass?" She made a face and turned in a quick circle, so he got the full benefit of the backless dress and the sweep of fabric over her ass. And since it didn't look like she wore any underwear...

He cleared his throat, willing away the heat that surged to his face. "Yes, you do. Please sit."

Ruby winked and seated herself gracefully, though she crossed her legs and the high heel she wore caught his attention. Delicate ankles and smooth, muscular calves... Carter shook himself out of his reverie and managed to get back to his chair, pouring her wine as he tossed the napkin across his lap to hide the evidence of how very well she passed. "You look lovely, Ruby."

"Thanks. You don't look so bad yourself." She gestured at the suit he wore, her lips slightly pursed. "I don't think I've ever seen you so dolled up."

"Only for special occasions." He smiled, but still wondered what game she played. This brash, up-front Ruby was just a show. The real Ruby, vulnerable and soft and willing, was the one he wanted to see. "Did you bring the records?"

"Of course." She pulled a manila envelope out of her bag and tossed it onto the table. "We need to expand the business, find other sources of income. So far everything we've considered has too high a cost of entry, and we can't get the financial backing to start up."

"What about loans?" He paged through the spreadsheets and detailed business plans, only half paying attention to what he read.

"We have enough debt with the bar. And we don't take charity, so don't offer. Nat already tried to convince me to take on Logan as a business partner, but the pack's business remains separate. That's just how it's going to be." She toyed with the delicate strand of pearls she wore, a ladylike accessory at odds with the tough tattoos and piercings.

Carter raised an eyebrow at her as he looked up. "So you turn down alternate sources of funding but complain about not having enough money to expand?"

Ruby folded her arms over her chest. "Rafe and I built this pack from nothing. We can take it to the next level without a hand-out."

He put the paperwork away as the waiter approached, and the business of ordering dinner distracted him from the way her cleavage beckoned. Only after the waiter retreated and Carter refilled her glass of wine did he go on. He studied her, the bravado as she surveyed the cozy but popular restaurant. "Where do you see yourself in a year, Ruby? In five years?"

Half her mouth pulled up in a smile, then Ruby leaned back and tapped a rhythmic pattern on the white tablecloth. "In a year? Probably still running the bar. Holding Evershaw off from taking over the pack."

"I meant where you *want* to be in a year. What are your goals? Good financial planning starts with a goal in mind. What do you want to accomplish?"

She got a faraway look and bit her lower lip. "I want to have the only pack in this city. I want to have the bar, a couple of restaurants, a gym, a hotel, everything. I want enough money so the people I love won't have to work shitty jobs anymore. I want to shut down the Auction so no more women are bartered away as if they were property."

"Noble goals." Carter leaned his elbows on the table, just to be closer to her. Just to catch a hint of the perfume she wore, maddening and intoxicating and curling around his brain until he couldn't think of anything but her. "But those are all for the pack. What are your personal goals?"

Her smile twisted into something sad and amused. "The pack is all that matters, Carter. You know that."

He shook his head. "Ruby, you deserve to be happy, to have goals of your own. The pack shouldn't be your entire life."

"You don't understand." She looked away, a hint of red in her eyes. But when she looked back at him and picked up her wine glass, her expression returned to smiling and dismissive. "Being alpha is all I ever wanted. Now, I've got it. I don't have the right to want more. Everything I have, everything I am – it goes to the pack."

Carter studied the tendril of hair that escaped the ponytail and curled near her ear, and he reached across the table to touch her hand without thinking. "I never understood why Logan wanted to be alpha, why he was so desperate to be in charge. It doesn't seem like a good thing, frankly. It's a burden and a punishment. He suffers for us. He suffers *because* of us. Our hurts are his hurts, but there's no one to care when he's hurting. It seems to me a terribly lonely way to live."

"I have Rafe." But she looked away.

His fingers closed around hers, the lion desperate to comfort her. "You deserve so much more, Ruby."

The silence stretched as she refused to look at him, and Carter refused to release her hand. He could be stubborn too, a quality his brothers despaired of. Eventually, she cleared her throat and straightened her shoulders, blue eyes calm as she tugged her hand free. "Strange conversation for a business meeting, Chase."

"I never said it was a business meeting."

Before she could retort, the waiter arrived with the first course. Carter wanted to break the silence but couldn't quite decide how to start. Only a few bites into the salad, Ruby pushed the dish back and propped her chin on her hands, fixing him with an intense look. "Look. Of course I want a partner and a mate. Of course I want kids and family and a loud house and hockey gear in the front hall, and toys in the yard, and everything. I want that. But I don't think I want that enough to give up what I've worked and sacrificed for, nor do I want that enough to screw my brother over and drive him away from what *he's* worked so hard for."

"Why does it mean —"

"Any wolf in this city that I would consider a partner would not be willing to tolerate Rafe as alpha." She shook her head, rubbing her forehead. "And if the guy *is* willing to let Rafe be alpha, then chances are I'm not going to be interested in him. So it's unfortunate, and yes, probably sad, but that's the reality."

"Why does he have to be a wolf?"

She opened her mouth to retort but stopped and her teeth clicked together. Carter raised his eyebrows. "Well? I know the wolves have rather draconian rules about a lot of things. Is it required that an alpha have a wolf mate?"

"It's not required."

"So why are you only choosing the scenario where you have to pick one or the other – the pack or a mate? Why not both?"

"Because that's not how it —"

He leaned forward and kept his voice low. "What are you afraid of, Ruby?"

"That I'll actually love you," she said, and he blinked.

Ruby cursed and looked away, across the restaurant, as the waiters brought a dessert tray around to another table. He waited, heart jumping to his throat. After a long pause, she glanced at him sideways. "Do you have any idea how scary it is to admit a weakness?"

"Of course." He leaned back as the waiter cleared their plates and replaced the salad with fragrant soup. When they were alone again, Carter rested his fingers on the edge of the table to keep from grabbing her hands again. "But there's no reason this is a weakness, Ruby. It's not —"

"It is for a woman." Her expression hardened. "Especially for a woman in charge. The moment I want to dress up, the moment I go on a date or hold hands with a guy — something changes. I become just another woman to be sheltered and coddled. Not the alpha, not the best fighter in the pack, not one of the most powerful wolves in the city. No, I'm just Carter's girlfriend. Me caring about someone? That's absolutely a weakness. *And* it's a weakness because what if you decide you don't want me? What if I like you more than you like me?"

Carter wanted to shake his head and smack his forehead. What a screwed up perspective on love. But it didn't entirely surprise him. The wolves in particular viewed everything as a zero sum game. Which made love and relationships competitions as well, in which one partner always had to have an advantage. She chewed her lower lip in a rare display of uncertainty, fidgeting with her silverware and reaching for the wine once more. "It might be too much of a leap for me. I don't know if I can deal with the uncertainty."

"But it would be easier to shack up with Evershaw?"

She made a face and tasted the soup, picked at the breadsticks, rearranged her napkin. Did anything and everything to not look at him. "At least with him, I know it wouldn't ever…my heart wouldn't get broken. Wouldn't even be in danger. It would be a power struggle every day for the rest of my life, but he wouldn't be able to hurt me as much as someone I care about."

Carter wanted to shake some sense into her. Imagine, picking an exhausting life of power struggles over a peaceful relationship. He scrubbed at his hair, not caring if it stood up in spikes and looked ridiculous. The lion grumbled about wanting to show her that no one would hurt her, not even him. *Especially* not him. Carter took a deep breath. "Aren't you tired, Ruby? You're vigilant all the time. Every minute. Don't you ever relax? Do you even sleep, or is one eye open all night?"

"Four or five hours," she said, with a half smile.

"Then why the hell don't you want to be with someone who can protect you while you sleep? Someone you can relax around, not because you're weak, but because I can be strong for both of us?"

She shook her head but didn't speak, once more concentrating on the utensils, and sadness gathered in her eyes. Irritated, Carter folded his napkin on the table and shoved to his feet. He held out his hand as she looked up. "Let's dance."

"Dance?"

He canted his head at the dance floor and the house band, a string quartet with a few extra pieces. "Dance. Come on."

Ruby scowled at him, but she tossed her napkin on the table. She would never turn down a challenge. She rose slowly and placed her hand in his, and Carter immediately pulled her to his side and set the pace to the dance floor. He needed contact with her, and the lion desperately needed to feel her skin. She was upset and sad, and the lion just wanted to take her some place warm, tuck her in, and curl up around her so she could sleep safely. The lead violinist smiled broadly when he saw them approach, clearly pleased someone would dance, and even raised his eyebrows to indicate Carter could choose the next song.

He smiled, said, "Tango, please," and was rewarded by an indignant sound from Ruby.

The soft waltz trailed off, wrapped up, and then the violinist slid into a beautiful Argentine tango. Carter faced Ruby as she hissed, "I don't know how to tango."

He took her left hand and placed it on his shoulder, and slid his right hand high on her back, her skin smooth and soft and warm under his palm. The scent of her hair distracted him as he pulled her close to his chest and his cheek brushed hers. "Luckily, I do. And since I'm leading, that works for us both."

She started to say something but instead he moved into the dance, the footwork coming naturally even though she jumped to catch up. Her face reddened and her eyes widened, and Ruby again started to chastise him, so Carter dipped her.

She laughed in surprise and some of the other patrons started to pay attention. Ruby's fingers dug into his shoulder as he whipped her back up and spun her out to the end of his grip. She gave him a look, and he winked before yanking her back toward him. Carter breathed her in, reveled in the feeling of her pressed against him, the way her breath caught when his hand at her back and the rest of his body prevented her from taking the lead. She wanted to lead – he could feel it with practically every step. Especially on the slow part of the dance, when they were pressed face to face– she tried for distance or to force him to go contrary to the dance. But he met every challenge and led her through every beat, occasionally letting himself appreciate the soft strength of her body and the hint of vanilla perfume. His lion purred, very low so it blended in with the music, but he knew she heard it.

As he pulled her close once more, her cheek brushed his and she whispered, "Kaiser said you were more dangerous for me than Evershaw. I think he's right."

Carter moved through the dance and then carefully dipped her once more as the tango ended, so he was looking down at her as the applause started and he could say, "Love is uncertain, not dangerous."

"You don't love me," she said, but she blushed as he pulled her upright and smiled at the other patrons. A few others decided to try the dance floor, so Carter led the way back to their table.

He pulled out her chair and studied her flushed cheeks, the way her hands trembled as she reached for her napkin. His fingers trailed across her forearm as he went back to his seat, the faint sound of her pulse thrumming in her throat distracting him. "How do you know?"

"Carter." The way she said his name, half laughing and half exasperated, drove him crazy. Drove the lion almost into a frenzy. He wanted to hear her say his name with breathy moans of desperation, calling for him to take her. Ruby didn't seem to notice, only shaking her head. "In literally a day and a half, you decide you love me?"

“I’ve loved you a lot longer than that,” he said, more than a little nervous that admitting this would backfire on him. But nothing ventured, nothing gained. He just prayed the waiter didn’t interrupt again. “I chose not to say something because you focused on the pack and building your business and it wasn’t a good time.”

“What changed?”

He tried not to smile. “You did.”

Ruby snorted but patted under her eyes quickly, shaking her head. “Now I know you’re crazy.”

“Crazy about you, maybe.” Carter sipped his wine and just watched her, content to have her close.

She couldn’t tolerate the unfilled silence and abruptly stood. “Excuse me for a moment.”

He half-stood from the table as she turned on her heel and marched toward the ladies’ room, and Carter watched her go. She still projected confidence. She owned that room, and only deigned to let everyone else sit there because she didn’t mind. He smiled and ordered another bottle of wine.

chapter 7

I thanked my lucky stars there wasn't a bathroom attendant, so at least I could pee and compose myself in peace. The tango stayed with me, though – the feeling of Carter's hand on my back, the strength in him as he took control and led through the dance. My heart still raced from the music, the warmth of his body, the scent of his cologne.

I paced inside the bathroom, unable to look at myself in the mirror. I'd bought the black dress months ago for a formal event but never wore it. I chickened out at the last minute and wore an old standby outfit, much more utilitarian and far less sexy. Some fit of craziness had me pull the sexy black dress, low cut and clingy, out of the back of the closet for my date with Carter.

"Stupid, stupid, stupid," I chanted, squeezing my eyes shut. I'd planned to break it off, to tell Carter it wouldn't work and we shouldn't even pretend to give this a shot. But part of me wanted what he offered. He was right, at least. A non-wolf wouldn't challenge my status in the pack. I took a deep breath and tried to get myself together. Just because he wasn't a wolf didn't mean this would work. He made me vulnerable. He made me think and do things I wouldn't normally do, and that would jeopardize my standing with the pack. It would give Evershaw another way to undermine us in front of the Council and the rest of the wolves. Publicly dating Carter could be the beginning of the end.

Except he said he loved me. Said he'd loved me for a while but didn't dare say anything. My mouth dried as panic surged in my chest. He loved me. Carter Chase loved me. Quiet, sweet, Carter. Who actually looked at the spreadsheets I'd brought from the bar. Who asked me to dance, and stood up from the table when I fled like a coward. Polite Carter, who never boasted, or blustered, or beat his chest to get attention. Who was fine with not being alpha — who didn't *want* to be alpha. I couldn't swallow.

It didn't make sense, he and I being together. It didn't. Edgar, maybe. But Carter was too nice. I washed my hands for the second time to buy time to think. I hated feeling so off-balance, and I knew if I went back to the table without getting my shit together, I'd say or do something I would regret later. But my thoughts kept drifting back to the feeling of being in his arms, his hips and shoulders whirling us across the dance floor. It had been a long time since I felt so delicate and protected. Charmed.

"Get it together," I told myself in the mirror. For fuck's sake, I was the alpha of BloodMoon pack. I couldn't afford to be indecisive and off-balance. Make a decision. Just make a decision and commit to it. I wanted to splash water on my face to knock some sense into me, but didn't dare.

I double-checked my cleavage in the mirror, glanced over my shoulder to make sure the dress wasn't tucked in itself and leaving my ass hanging out, and strode back into the restaurant. I could handle this.

But as I approached the table and Carter stood once more to pull out my chair, my resolve and my knees wobbled. He looked like perfection in his tailored suit. Like arm candy I'd custom-ordered, with sandy blonde hair and milk chocolate eyes and a mischievous half-smile that made my heart speed up. Damn it. And for the first time, my wolf sat up and took notice. She liked him, too. Wanted him to chase us.

Heat rushed to my face as I sat, muttering a thank you to him, and I braced my hands on the table as I stared down at my plate. My resolve wavered as I looked up.

Carter nodded at the food. "They just brought the entrees, so everything should be hot. If it isn't, I'll call him back."

I didn't want to talk about the food, but my stomach rumbled and I cut into the steak. Maybe a little protein would magic up some fortitude for me. He watched me as he tasted his own food, and for a moment, his mouth distracted me, and I wondered what it would feel like to have his lips pressed against my throat. On my breasts, my stomach.

I cleared my throat and tried not to think of that as I patted my lips with the napkin. "Here's the thing."

His smile grew a touch, and he arranged the utensils on his plate. "Oh?"

"I like you, too." The words slipped out before I could second-guess myself as my heart tried to break through my ribs. Even though he'd already said he loved me, admitting I liked him as well still terrified the shit out of me. I gripped the table so I wouldn't fly apart from nervous energy. "And I think…I think I want to give this a try. But there have to be rules. I have to protect my pack first, and everything else comes second."

Carter frowned in thought as he studied me, head tilted to the side. "I would never do anything to harm your pack, Ruby."

God, I loved when he said my name. It made shivers run all the way through me, landing like a caress against my thigh. "Not deliberately. But things happen. If people know we're close, they might try to use you against me. Or use you to get to me. So I'd rather we have a…trial run. Private. Not openly be together but try it out to see if it might actually work."

"I don't like the idea of keeping secrets from my family or yours," he said. "And while I understand your hesitation, I've had enough experience keeping people away from Logan and Edgar that I'm pretty sure I'll recognize if someone tries to use me to get to you."

"Please," I said, and hated the uncertainty. I wanted him. I wanted to feel like I had during the tango, when his heart beat against my chest, his fingers were rough on my back, his legs turning and twisting me until I was totally lost. I wanted to be tangled up with him, wanted the promise of what he'd said the night before – letting someone else take control. Letting *him* take control. I took a deep breath. "Carter, I need a little time before I go public. Okay? If only to figure out the pack stuff."

"I'll go with it," he said, rubbing his jaw. "But we should set a time limit, okay? Give it two weeks, and if we're still in it, we go public. If not, we agree to part ways, no feelings hurt, and nothing left unsaid. Agreed?"

"Agreed." I finished the rest of my wine and loved him even more when he picked up the new bottle to refill my glass. Bless his little heart. Liquid courage helped me get the next part out. "And I don't want you to interfere in any pack business."

"Why would you think I would —"

"Because I know how you lions work." I leveled a no-bullshit look at him. "And if something comes up, you won't be able to help yourself if you think your mate is in trouble. Except the second you involve yourself on my behalf, you undermine my standing in the pack. You absolutely cannot…what?"

He'd started smiling and heat kindled in his gaze. "If my *mate* is in trouble, no, I won't be able to help myself."

Shit. I swallowed an immediate denial and fumbled for new words, furious with myself that he could put me so off-balance with just a look. My wolf didn't mind. She wanted to test how much he wanted us. "You know what I meant, Carter."

"I do." His smile twitched a little wider even as he tried to hide it behind his wine glass. "And I promise I won't interfere with any of your pack business. Unless your life is threatened. Then, I will absolutely do everything in my power to defend you, and there is nothing in the universe you could say that would convince me to watch you die. Mates protect each other."

My cheeks burned. I looked away as a knot grew in my throat. After getting accustomed to every single man I ran into being a threat, or a challenge, or just an obstacle, to have him say with such calm confidence that I was his mate and he would protect me, shifted the foundation under me. He re-set the world with just a sentence and a smile. I cleared my throat and managed to go on. "Fine. But I can't have you interfering with pack business, especially since Logan is so involved with the Council. If there's a dispute, I stand on my own."

He sighed and sat back in his chair. "Ruby, you're killing me. What good am I as a mate unless I can stand *with* you?"

"I need to know you're..." I trailed off, uncertain. I rubbed my temples and leaned forward, dropping my voice in case any shifters were mixed in among the humans, and someone might overhear. "I don't need an attack dog, Carter. Rafe is that. He stands beside me when I need to be a total bitch and alpha over the pack, and with the rest of the Council. What I need more, what I need from...you is...a safe place, a soft place to land. Some place where I can relax, where I can be weak or hurt or sad and not have to conceal it. Not have to hide anything. I need someone who will take care of me, and shelter me, and not resent it. Won't lord it over me in public or make jokes about it in front of his friends. I don't know if that's you, if that's something you want to take on, but —"

"I don't know how it is with you wolves," he said, interrupting me so calmly I blinked instead of firing back about him being a rude lion. "But lions groom to show affection. We provide food to show love. We build dens and soft nests for our families."

A knot grew in my throat and my sinuses seemed to have caught fire.

He leaned forward, large hands resting on the table next to mine – not touching, but close enough if I wanted. His voice rumbled in his chest, practically a purr, as he went on. "Since you're upset right now and I don't entirely understand why, I want to take you to my den. I want to run you a hot bath, and get in there with you and clean you. Soap you up until you smell like me. Take you to my bed and put you in it, and sleep next to you. Sleep on top of you so no one will ever hurt you. And then make you food and watch you eat every bite. Give you my clothes to wear. Nap all day long in the hammock on the porch when the sun is just right. Give you a soft place to rest whenever you want it."

My heart thumped. My hands shook a little as I reached for my wine, wondering if I was out of my mind. "Is that all you would do with me?"

The smile fell away but the heat remained in his eyes, until they practically threw sparks. His voice dropped as he touched my fingers. "Not at all, but I don't know if that falls into the 'soft place to land' category. That's more along the lines of the 'nice kind of spanking' or the 'fuzzy restraints instead of handcuffs'. Just so you know."

I clenched my thighs against a surge of desire as I imagined him taking me across his knee and spanking my bare ass, blindfolding me, tying my hands to the headboard so he could do whatever he wanted to me. I swallowed and tried for nonchalance. "I'm not sure that —"

"You're turned on by just the thought," he said under his breath, drinking more wine as the waiter approached to ask about dessert. Carter didn't take his eyes off me as he said to the man, "We'll take two of the berries sabayon. To go."

My heart climbed to my throat. As soon as the waiter retreated, Carter leaned across the table to murmur, "I'll be eating most of my dessert off you, but if you want to try yours, you'll have to be a very good girl."

I laughed, more from surprise than amusement, and pressed the tips of my fingers to my mouth to hold the sound back. I managed to say, "I'm not usually good."

"That's okay," he said. He even winked. "More fun for me if you're not."

I choked on the sip of wine I'd dared, and braced myself on the table as I coughed. When he said things like that, I almost couldn't reconcile him with the Carter who just said he wanted to draw me a hot bath and make me breakfast.

My voice turned into a croak as I tried to take control back. "My place or yours?"

"Since you don't want the family to know, my place isn't an option. And it's thirty minutes back to the mansion. Your place is closer, but I'm guessing the walls aren't sound-proof."

"No, they're not." I rested my chin on my fist, watching him. This was insane. Absolutely insane. "But I don't really like my neighbors, so I don't mind if we keep them up."

He shook his head in mock disappointment. "So rude and inconsiderate. We might have to adjust your attitude, Ruby."

And again my heart thrilled, my insides tingled, my skin prickled. All I could think of was that tango. The wolf demanded we bite him. Cut to the chase and mark him so every other bitch in the city would know this one was off-limits. We might play around with him and pretend we were helpless, but if anyone looked at him twice, we'd defend our claim. When I smiled, I showed all my teeth so he'd know I meant it.

chapter 8

Carter drove back to Ruby's apartment as she sat quiet in the seat next to him and held the to-go boxes. Even though the apartment was only a couple of blocks away, it felt like an eternity. She smelled so damn good he could barely keep his hands on the wheel. A hint of lust wafted from her and curled through his senses, driving the lion to near madness. As soon as he started telling her what to do, she got a glint in her eyes that promised a hell of a night. The steering wheel creaked in his grip.

Her phone rang and she answered, listening before she said, "Just leaving dinner. Carter looked at the records. He's going to come up with a plan."

He'd promised no such thing, but she slid him a sideways look and bit her lip, so he knew he would. Carter nodded, trying to hide his smile, and concentrated on the road. She lived downtown, but on the edge of safe neighborhoods. He wondered why she didn't just live over the bar with Rafe. Although he was grateful she didn't, since they would have had to get a hotel room and explaining that to Logan might have gotten dicey.

Still, he'd meant it when he talked about making her a safe den. And the neighborhood where she lived was not safe. After the two weeks, they'd find some place nicer. A place for both of them, together. He was tired of living in the mansion full-time, and wanted to escape to the city when he needed space.

Ruby shifted in the seat and the skirt of that sexy dress rode up, exposing more of her creamy white thigh. A hint of a tattoo teased. Carter focused on parking the car next to a moderately crappy apartment building. He liked that dress. He really didn't want to ruin it, but his lion wanted to shred the fabric until every naked inch of her was exposed. Covered in berries and chocolate and whipped cream – his dessert.

A growl escaped before he could control himself, and Ruby started to grin. Her fingers trailed across the back of his hand, sending a shock through his entire body. "Penny for your thoughts?"

He put the car in park, killed the engine, and leaned over to drag her mouth to his. He kissed her, hungry, and she made a soft sound and braced her hand against his shoulder. His growl increased as he tasted her, felt the slick heat of her tongue against his, and slid his hand up her side to her cleavage, warm and soft against his palm. Ruby reached for him and almost dumped the dessert on the floorboard. Carter broke the kiss and sat back, struggling to sound normal as he opened his door. "Sorry. Didn't have any pennies."

He took a deep breath of the cool night air, ran a hand through his hair, and walked around the car to open her door. She hadn't bothered to wait, and was half out of the car already. Carter fought back irritation but captured her hand and tucked it in the crook of his arm, keeping her warm for the walk up to her apartment. The wind caught her perfume and it tangled in his brain. He could hear her heart racing as she jiggled the key in the lock and shoved the door open, and he followed close behind.

Inside, Ruby turned on a few lights and tossed her house keys on a side table on her way into the galley kitchen, still carrying the boxes of dessert. Carter locked the door and set the deadbolt and chain, taking in the moderately priced furniture and generic artwork. Nothing cheap, but nothing too expensive. He was willing to bet she saved the quality furnishings for her pack, and lived with the leftovers as good enough. He wanted more for her. Much, much more.

Ruby returned from the kitchen to hand him a bottle of water, her hips swaying in the fancy dress. She leaned against the wall and fiddled with her shoes, her eyes gold as she watched him. "These damn…"

"Leave them on."

She went still and heat sparked in her gaze. Carter's voice came out deep and rough, and he set the water aside. His hands flexed. "Come here."

Her breasts rose and fell as her breath came faster, but she swayed forward the few steps until she stood in front of him. Waiting. Carter wanted to rip the dress off her, take her to bed with her heels on. But he picked up her wrist, studying her hand and fingers. "This is about trust, Ruby. You have to trust me. Do you?"

Her lips parted and her pupils dilated as he kissed the inside of her wrist, and her pulse jumped against his lips. She touched her throat with her free hand, expression dreamy but a touch uncertain. "Yes."

Carter smiled and caught her other hand to hold her wrists captive. He leaned in to brush his lips to hers, and trailed kisses down her throat to her shoulder. She swayed against him, sighing, and turned her face to breathe against his cheek. Carter nibbled behind her ear, reaching up with his free hand to tug her hair free of the ponytail, and the dark locks cascaded around him with a honeysuckle scent. He inhaled it, inhaled her. "Pick a word to use, if you want to stop for any reason."

Her voice went a little high as he caught her lower back and pressed her to him, until she felt the strength of his desire against her hip. The lion growled and grumbled, furious with the delay. Carter kissed the other side of her neck, dragging his teeth across a tribal tattoo on her shoulder, and she tried to link her arms around him. He kept her wrists caught between them, despite that she tugged on his grip, and nipped at the soft flesh where her shoulder met her neck. "Pick a word."

Ruby laughed breathlessly. "Glacier. Does that work?"

"Perfect." He wished he'd been more prepared but necessity was the mother of invention. He stepped back and released her, even though Ruby swayed toward him, and loosened his tie. "Get some candles. Matches. And the dessert. Go to the bedroom and wait for me."

She eyed him, about to speak, but he patted her hip and pointed her toward the bedroom. "Go."

He watched her saunter to a linen closet to retrieve some candles and matches, then she picked up the boxes from the kitchen, and made her back once more past him. Carter wanted to grab her but resisted, instead looking through the coat closet near the door for a scarf or two. When he found what he wanted, he followed Ruby into the bedroom.

She'd left the lights off but lit the candles, and she stood at the end of the bed, hands on her hips. So much attitude. He fought back a smile and tossed the scarves onto a nearby chair. He took off his jacket and tie, studying her in the flickering shadows, then pointed at a spot on the floor directly in front of him. "Come here."

Ruby obeyed and his heart jumped, his cock painfully hard. Watching her submit, or at least pretend to, was so fucking arousing he almost needed to excuse himself. She bit her lower lip as she looked at him, almost taunting. Carter brushed her hair back over her shoulders so he could examine her, walking a slow circle around her as he played with one of the scarves.

Carter leaned closer and breathed against the bare skin of her neck, making a hungry noise in his throat. Her breath caught. He trailed his fingers across her shoulder as he stood behind her, playing with the zipper at the back of her dress. Ruby tensed as he worked the zipper and the dress fell to the floor in a dark cascade. He caressed her lower back and ran his finger under the waist of her thong. She shivered.

He almost couldn't breathe. Perfection. She was absolute perfection — soft, smooth skin decorated with a multitude of tattoos over gentle curves. The lacy black bra and silky hose drove him wild, almost as wild as the high heels. He stepped back to appreciate her, and when the silence stretched and he said nothing, she shifted her feet. "Are you —"

"Don't speak." Carter knew it would drive her crazy, so he let the scarf brush her shoulder. She jumped at the touch, about to turn, but froze as he slapped her hip. Ruby made a needy noise instead but didn't move. Carter eased the scarf over her eyes and began to tighten it. She inhaled sharply so he paused, standing close behind her so she could feel his presence, and whispered in her ear. "All you have to do is say that word and we stop."

He could sense the tension in her, the desperate wanting to move or speak or take control. But instead she only gave a small shake of her head and exhaled. He finished tying the scarf around her eyes, made sure it was secure, then ran his hands over her shoulders to her breasts. "Good girl."

She chewed her lower lip as he moved around to the front, studying her once more. He leaned to lick her breasts through the lace bra, using the rough fabric to tease her nipples to hardness. Her chest rose and fell faster and her lips parted to allow panting breaths to escape. He watched a flush turn her skin rosy. Carter's hand grazed her stomach and she jumped. He eased the thong down her lush thighs until it caught around her ankles, and knelt to remove it entirely. He didn't want her to trip when things got exciting.

He breathed against her stomach and ran his hands up the insides of her legs, easing them apart, and she gasped. Carter stroked the length of her damp slit, chuckling as he straightened. "Ready so soon, Ruby?"

Her lips curved but he didn't give her a chance to reply. Instead he crushed her mouth to his in a deep, demanding kiss, one hand tight in her hair to maintain control as he walked her back to the mattress. He lay her out on the mattress and took off his shirt and pants before reaching for one of the candles. Things were about to get messy.

chapter 9

The blindfold heightened every one of my senses until I trembled in anticipation. Not being able to see him but feeling the air move as he did and hearing the hush-hush of his breath... I almost couldn't stand it. Heat rushed to my center and radiated through me until my knees wobbled and I thought I might fall on my face. And then when he took off my thong and hose, when he kissed my stomach and pressed his hand against my pussy, I nearly came.

When he put me on the bed I wanted to resist, to tear off the blindfold and demand he fuck me, but the night promised so much more. The mattress depressed next to me and Carter's palms moved over my lace-covered breasts. He kissed my throat and murmured, "You have to stay very still for this part, my dear. Do I need to tie you up or will you behave yourself?"

I clenched my thighs together and bit back a moan. I'd never been so turned on in my life. I even sounded breathless as I answered him. "I don't know."

He chuckled again, a husky sound that sent shivers through me, and then soft fabric caught around my wrists as he dragged my arms over my head. "Very well."

Being restrained caused a moment of hesitation, reconsideration, and I started to struggle, but he kissed me softly and stroked my cheek. "Good girl. Very good."

My heart leapt as I kissed him back, desperate for more contact and more of his praise. Carter traced a snaking line down my chest and stomach until he teased my core, pressing his thumb against my clit even as his finger eased inside me. My back arched and I tried to reach for him but the restraints stopped me short.

He grumbled again, almost laughing, then retreated. The bed felt cold and empty without him. When he didn't return, a hint of panic welled up. What if he left? What if he was just fucking with me and this was all a joke? My breath came faster and I moved uneasily, heels digging into the mattress to see if I could unhook my hands from wherever he'd secured them.

But then a palm collided with my thigh in a sharp slap and I jumped. Carter sounded stern. "Don't. Move."

Just knowing he was close gave me the courage to remain still, though I held my breath. Something else was coming. He prepared something. And as he moved next to me, over me, I clenched my hands around the soft scarf.

Something burned against the tops of my breasts in a slow series of droplets. A sharp pain that faded, but with each drop, the pain spiked more intense. I gasped, trembling as the drops ceased — then started lower, across my stomach, and I cried out. The candles. It had to be the candles. Hot wax heightened every sensation, even more as he teased my nipples, until I nearly went mad with desire. I wanted him, *needed* him. I panted, out of breath from moaning and begging, and Carter's hands ghosted up my sides.

"Do you like that, Ruby?" he murmured, the rough stubbed on his jaw riding against my sensitive flesh until a strangled noise caught in my throat.

"Y-yes," I managed to breathe, staring into the blindfold as if I could see through it to find where he would touch me next.

"Good." He practically purred and something soft stroked over my thigh. My legs fell open in anticipation and he laughed. "Is there something you want, Ruby?"

"You," I whispered. "I want you, Carter, I need you so —"

"Not yet." Another line of fire erupted low on my stomach and I cried out.

The teasing and torment continued, alternating soft kisses and gentle touching with hot wax and the occasional teeth on my nipples, until I writhed and begged. Madness. He drove me to the edge, until I thought I would explode from needing to come, and then Carter would back off, leaving me trembling and helpless.

Just when I couldn't take it, when I ached to say the word to stop it all, his palm chafed my hip and he lifted my knee up and out. I almost cried in relief as his weight settled over me, though he held himself off my chest and nuzzled his nose to mine. Carter kissed me and took my lower lip in his teeth. "And now I have you, exactly how I wanted."

"Please," I said, pulling weakly at the scarf. "Carter, please."

The tip of his cock stroked against my core, up to my clit, and I came. Hard. Arched against him and convulsed, crying out and shaking and falling apart in a thousand pieces. The world grew darker behind the blindfold and I couldn't have lifted my arms for anything in the world. His massive cock nudged inside me and I moaned, pushing my hips at him, and Carter pushed forward with slow inevitability. He split me open, the heavy heat of his body invading mine until he filled every inch of me, pressed against my walls until pleasure rippled through me and I tumbled into ecstasy again.

It blended into almost unbearable pleasure, unbelievable fullness until it sparked a hint of pain. And that brought the pleasure-pain of the hot wax back until I could hardly remain in my own skin. Carter moved slowly but lowered himself on top of me until his full weight lay on my chest and I was pinned, dominated. Utterly controlled, even had my hands been free. I couldn't have moved him if I wanted. It drove me wild, to the point of madness as I pushed my hips at him in desperation, needing fuller contact. More thrusting. I begged him and tried to hook my legs around his lower back to drag him to me, but Carter spanked my hip with his full strength and I cried out even as it made my pussy clench around him once more.

Carter breathed in my ear, "I'll have to punish you for that," and I groaned and came again.

By the time he moved with more urgency, I could barely move. Exhausted and covered in sweat and wax, I surrendered and opened myself to him. To everything. Let him move my legs and hips and body to where he liked until he grunted and pounded into me with a wet slapping of flesh that had my head rolling on the pillows. He froze, hips jerking and grinding down against me, and the hot rush of his climax filled me, spilled out, covered my thighs. I panted, helpless and trapped underneath him, but loving the security of having him over me. I closed my eyes but couldn't stop shaking.

Carter withdrew and I flinched at the sensation of his body slipping from mine, and I missed him immediately. Wanted desperately to have him over me, inside me, again. Forever. But he remained next to me on the bed, fiddling with the scarf, and then he eased my arms down to my sides, chafing at my wrists and hands. I took a breath to say something, to beg him for more, but he touched my lips to cut me off. "You don't want to add to your punishment, my dear."

I shivered, almost tempted to push, but that could wait for another night. I could hardly support myself as Carter moved me to my hands and knees, though my thighs clenched in anticipation and my elbows shook with the effort of holding my chest off the bed. He left the blindfold on me, so I could feel him next to my hips but had no idea what he planned until his palm cracked against my ass. I jumped away from the painful spanking but he grabbed a handful of my hair with his free hand to hold me in place and leaned down to say, "Hold still or I will start over."

My head hung down and I struggled to remain unmoving as he landed another blow on my ass, and a cry escaped even as my pussy clenched. God help me, I loved it. Wanted to lean into it as he continued raining blows down, until my skin radiated heat and I thought I might never be able to sit down again. He chuckled and ran his fingers through my pussy once more, pinching and teasing, then knelt behind me to grasp my waist. His cock filled me in a single thrust and I wailed, convulsing around him as the pleasure of his entry competed with the aching throb of his spanking. Carter fucked me from behind, leaning over my back to hold me roughly in place, and he growled against my shoulder as I struggled to hold up our combined weight.

He teased my clit but I didn't need it to come; it felt like I hadn't stopped coming from the moment he'd touched me. Like it had built from the first bars of the tango and all exploded through me as he yanked off the blindfold and I looked up to see both of us in the mirror over my dresser.

His wild expression, teeth bared, as he thrust, the dark outline where our bodies connected, and the helpless passion on my face sent me over the edge again. Carter snarled and put his arm under my chest, holding me tight to him as he fucked down at me. I could only watch helplessly in the mirror as I came and he came and we both collapsed on the bed in a sweaty tangle.

When our breathing slowed, Carter patted my hip. "And now there's the matter of your punishment."

I laughed in disbelief, trying to find the strength to lift my head, but the glint in his eyes made my stomach wobble. He couldn't be serious.

Except he was. And Carter took punishments very seriously.

I stretched in the warm bed, my hand sliding across the sheets, and I lifted my head enough to look around. No Carter. Memories of the night before and everything he'd done set my cheeks on fire, and I pulled the covers up over my face. Unbelievable.

Something rattled in the small apartment. I sat up, wincing at the ache in my abs, and eased to my feet. The speedy shifter healing got rid of most of the evidence of the bites, and restraints, and hot wax, but the thought of it stuck with me as I stretched. I pulled on a t-shirt before padding out of the bedroom and into the living room. Carter stood in the kitchen, juggling pans and plates and ingredients as he made pancakes and sausages, and I raised my eyebrows. "Don't tell me you're a morning person."

He glanced back with a devilish smile, and all my nerves lit up. I wanted to kiss him, drag him back to the bedroom, and let him tie me up again. His voice went deep and husky. "And if I am?"

I played with the hem of the t-shirt as I wandered into the kitchen and retrieved two glasses from the cupboard. "Well, I'll just have to..."

I cut off with a squeak as he grabbed me and pressed me up against the cabinets, biting my lip before kissing me until my knees weakened. I linked my arms around his neck just to stay upright, my bones melting as his hand slid inside my shirt to caress my breast. A moan escaped before I could control myself and he echoed it, hiking me up until my legs wrapped around his waist. Carter broke the kiss long enough to set his teeth against my shoulder, right near my neck as he squeezed my ass. "Normally I would stick around long enough to finish things, but it's already eight and I have a meeting with Logan at nine. And you're supposed to meet Natalia."

I moved my hips, dropping my head forward so I could bite his shoulder.

He groaned, then fumbled with the pants he'd pulled on, and before I could draw breath, he plunged into me. I cried out as Carter thrust, his hands gripping my ass to hold me still as his cock split me open, and the cabinets creaked under the force of his lust. My wolf snarled and wanted to mark him, to claim him, and my nails dug in to his biceps as he fucked me. The wildness overtook us both, and snarling filled the kitchen. I strained under his weight and strength pinning me, desperate to move. Carter slapped my hip with the full strength of his arm and I yelped, almost crawling up him, and ecstasy rolled over me. I froze as my core clamped down on him, and every movement of his body inside me sent lightning straight to my brain. Carter made a savage noise and his teeth sank into my shoulder with a sudden sharp pain, and I moaned. His body jerked against me and he went still, breathing harshly in my ear.

My heart pounded against my ribs and I rested my head against the cabinet behind me as I struggled to breathe. Jesus.

Carter eased back, and I took a sharp breath at the shock of his body slipping from mine. He handed me a dishtowel and leaned forward to kiss me again, gently, and murmured, "Go take a shower and get dressed. I'll have breakfast ready."

I leaned against the cabinets for a long moment, watching as he cleaned himself up and pulled his pants back on, then washed his hands. Carter glanced back at me, eyebrow arched, with a question in his expression. I flushed, not wanting to admit that I wasn't entirely certain my legs would hold me if I tried to walk to the bathroom. And by the way a grin spread across his face, he wondered the same thing.

I cleared my throat as I wobbled upright and turned on my heel, though I kept a good hand on the wall just in case. "See that you do."

He laughed. I barely made it to the shower, leaning against the wall as steam filled the small room, and I closed my eyes against the hot water. The lion was like an addiction. Even after the savage pounding in the kitchen, I still wanted him. I wanted him to kick open the door and drag me out of the shower by my hair. My skin prickled as I brushed my nipples and down my stomach, and I chewed my lip ragged as I focused on washing my hair and getting my equilibrium back. Maybe him being a lion and generally an easy-going guy wasn't the problem. Maybe me wanting to spend every waking moment in his bed would be the problem. I scrubbed at my face and shut off the water. I needed to get my shit together. Natalia would know in a heartbeat that something was off, and while I valued her opinion and advice, part of me wanted to keep what Carter and I had a secret. As soon as it went public, something would change. I didn't want to lose him yet.

I dressed as quickly as I could, the scent of pancakes and roasting sausage drawing me back to the kitchen. Besides, a man who cooked was pretty rare. One who cooked well was damn near a unicorn.

chapter 10

Carter stared at the spreadsheets in front of him, but his mind kept wandering back to Ruby. Her apartment, her kitchen in particular, crept back into his thoughts, despite how he tried to focus on work. He missed the first meeting with Logan, although that wasn't entirely his fault; his eldest brother also ran late. Something was up with Logan and Natalia, and though Carter had his suspicions, it wasn't his place to pry. Not until they decided to share the news.

He rubbed his forehead and picked up the spreadsheets again. He meant to develop a business plan for Ruby and Rafe so they could focus their efforts to expand, but unless they could take out a loan or would accept a Chase partner with some extra cash, there wasn't a whole lot he could recommend. Some cosmetic fixes, adjusting the current offerings, and advertising could help some, no doubt. The bar food was terrible unless Natalia moon-lighted in the kitchen, and they stocked the kind of beer that the pack liked — dark, bitter brews that appealed to only a small section of their non-shifter clientele. O'Shea's was a dive bar, and though he loved every square inch of it because it belonged to Ruby, she had caviar dreams for her pack.

Caviar. He frowned and spun his chair until he could stare out the window at the city below. He could cover her in caviar and then eat it off her. The dessert stuff was fun, but a man needed some protein to keep up his strength. He rubbed his mouth to hide a smile, then jumped as someone cleared their throat behind him.

Carter rotated to face Logan and Edgar. "Yes?"

Edgar picked up some of the spreadsheets, a frown creasing his forehead. "What are you working on?"

"Ruby and Rafe asked me to look at their financials. Work up a business plan." Carter prayed his voice remained even and no emotion showed on his face, particularly since the super observant Edgar eyed him closely. Carter leaned forward on the desk, banishing any thoughts of Ruby from his mind, and looked at his brothers. "You look serious. What happened?"

Logan flopped into one of the chairs in front of the desk, his expression dark. "I got a call from Kaiser. Apparently Miles Evershaw is reaching out to all the other shifters in the city, except us. What happened the other day at the gym?"

"What makes you think anything…"

"Nat dropped the dime on you." Logan arched an eyebrow. "But she didn't have any details other than that you bumped chests with Evershaw. Which is unlike you, Carter."

He pinched the bridge of his nose as Edgar continued to stand, arms folded over his chest. Carter could fake out Logan without too much trouble, but the security chief was another thing entirely. Carter sighed. "I went there after yoga to work out. Natalia and Ruby showed up and Ruby negotiated a group deal for her pack to the use the gym. Before they reached an agreement, Evershaw and half of his guys knocked on the door and started making trouble. There's something between him and Ruby right now, I don't know any details."

Edgar made a thoughtful noise and started to pace the long wall of the office, hands shoved in his pockets. "So why did you bump chests with Evershaw?"

"He tried some underhanded shit with Ruby, then Nat got between them, and he flexed on her."

Logan sat forward, eyes immediately gold. "He *what*?"

"I took care of it." Carter held up his hands to fend off the growing rage Logan radiated. "And put Nat out of harm's way. Then I stayed on Evershaw until Kaiser told him to back off. I knew if Evershaw got too aggressive with Ruby that Natalia wouldn't be able to keep from getting involved, so I got more involved than I intended."

The alpha narrowed his eyes as he gripped the arms of the chair. "Natalia conveniently left out the part where she got between two angry wolves. I will address that with her later."

Edgar snorted. "By address that, you mean you'll tell her not to do it again, and she'll laugh at you and say you won't stop her from doing what she wants, and then you'll grumble and whine and let her do what she wants? That kind of address?"

Logan gave him a dark look. "Save it for later, asshole." He turned his attention to Carter, but his eyes retained a hint of gold. "Evershaw threatened my mate?"

"Not exactly. He was an asshole to her, and she got between him and Ruby when they were about to fight."

Logan's teeth gleamed as he snarled, then he shoved to his feet to stalk the edges of the office. Carter took a deep breath and eased to his feet, just in case he and Edgar had to tackle their brother before Logan took off to go kill the SilverLine alpha. Carter said, "What did Kaiser tell you about Evershaw? Is SilverLine stirring up more trouble?"

"The bears think Evershaw is pushing to have a single representative for wolves on the Council, to be decided by a fight between SilverLine and BloodMoon." Edgar spoke but kept his eyes on Logan's jerky pacing and snarling. "And possibly that Evershaw wants to combine both packs. With himself as alpha, of course."

Carter's blood started a slow boil. He knew Evershaw was an underhanded asshole, but going to the Council to undermine Ruby and Rafe was a new low for the Silver-Line alpha. He gripped the edge of his desk until the wood creaked. "Do Ruby and Rafe know yet?"

"Probably not." Edgar watched him closely. "There's no reason Evershaw would include them in his machinations, and we only just heard from Kaiser. The bears want to call an emergency Council session tomorrow so we can discuss this. Without the wolves present."

Logan turned toward the door. "Good. Because then it will be at least two days before anyone knows I killed Evershaw."

Edgar grabbed his arm. "Whoa there, brother. Natalia is fine. Carter protected her, the bears protected her, I'm damn sure Ruby protected her. Take a deep breath or I'll send you to the gym again."

Carter moved around the desk so he could help if Logan made a run for it. "Again?"

"We've had a rough morning." Edgar smiled with half his mouth. "Natalia was up early to accept deliveries at the restaurant, and called our fearless leader in tears because the tomatoes were bruised."

Logan made a strangled sound and gripped double fistfuls of his hair, whirling on his heel to keep storming through Carter's office. "Those fucking tomatoes. Can we buy a tomato farm? Is there such a thing? How do I keep tomatoes from bruising?"

Edgar laughed but cut it off when Logan gave him a snarling gold-eyed look. The second-in-command held up his hands and chuckled. "Come on, dude. You can't be mad for that. How do you keep tomatoes from bruising? That's completely fucking irrational. I don't even know why she would be crying about…"

Carter held his breath as Logan lurched to a halt.

Edgar took a deep breath and gripped the back of a nearby chair, as if to steady himself. "Is she pregnant?"

Logan ground the heels of his hands into his eyes. "It's still early."

"Holy shit." Carter couldn't bite back a smile. "Logan, man, congratulations. That's fantastic."

Logan looked a little dazed. "It's still too early."

"It will be fine." Edgar clapped their brother on the back, then pulled him in for a hug. "Congratulations. You're going to be an amazing dad. When is she due?"

"I don't even know." Logan laughed, still shaking his head in pure confusion. "She's told me at least half a dozen times but I can't…May? I think it's May."

"Well," Carter said, leaning back against his desk. "That explains why you're ready to kill Evershaw. But what do we do about the Council?"

"There are a lot more reasons to get rid of Evershaw than just him being mean to Natalia," Logan said under his breath. He ran a hand through his hair, trying to get it to lie flat. "But I don't know. It almost makes sense to have a single representative for each group, but that also creates a lot more problems than it solves. I'm not sure I believe Evershaw that it's necessary."

"We'll see." Edgar glanced at his watch. "Logan, go back to your office. Natalia is at the dress place, so call and send her flowers or something. Or a car to take her to lunch. She said Ruby was meeting her there, so send them both something."

"Why?" Logan rubbed the back of his neck, looking around the office as if he'd never seen it before. "It's not an anniversary or…"

"Because she's the mother of your child, you fucking idiot." Edgar shoved him out the door. "Flowers *and* candy, just because you're useless. And don't tell your assistant to do it, make the call yourself." Then Edgar shut the door and faced Carter. "Okay, brother. Spill."

"What?"

"Don't play innocent." Edgar's head tilted as he studied Carter, a bit of hunting intensity in his gaze. "Something happened. You didn't go back to the house last night. You slept somewhere else, and you look guilty. What happened?"

Carter growled in irritation and returned to his desk. "I don't want to talk about it."

"A date went well? Really well?" And Edgar pointed to Carter's shoulder, where his shirt gapped and revealed a hint of a bite.

Carter immediately adjusted his collar and pretended to concentrate on the spreadsheets once more. "No. And I'm not going to talk about it."

"There's no shame in getting laid." Edgar folded his arms over his chest. "Just give us a head's up when it gets serious."

"It's not going to get serious," Carter said under his breath, shaking his head as he focused on the paperwork. He regretted it immediately, because Edgar never let things like that go past unexamined.

"Why not?"

"She's skittish." It was the only word to describe Ruby's commitment issues. "About relationships. So messing around is fine as long as no one else knows, but if we were to go public…that's problematic. And that's all I'm going to say about it, and her, so don't ask me."

"Carter…"

"Please, Edgar. Don't ask." Carter stared at his desk with enough intensity he expected it to burst into flames. His lion wanted to race into the city, find Ruby, and make things permanent. Show her she couldn't live without him, and he couldn't live without her. Thinking she would walk away from him felt more like a punch in the balls than just harmless speculation.

At length, Edgar took a deep breath. "Is she your mate?"

Carter looked at his desk, but didn't see any of the normally comforting consistency of numbers. Just a blurry mess and Ruby's face underneath it all, taunting him. "Yeah."

"And you're going to let her walk away?"

He managed to look up at Edgar, willing all pain and expression from his face. "If she chooses something else over me, what choice do I have? I'm not going to kidnap her and drag her away. We've never been bride-nappers."

"What *choice*?" Edgar's eyes glinted cold gray, more like steel than storm clouds. "For fuck's sake, Carter, if she's your mate, you show her there *is* no other choice. What could she choose over you? What would make her life more complete, more secure, more perfect, than *you*? That's your job."

Carter rubbed his forehead and slowly leaned back in his chair, turning to stare out the window so maybe Edgar wouldn't be able to read his expression so easily. "She'll choose her pack over me, Ed, in a heartbeat. And I knew that going in. I just couldn't stand to let another day go by without touching her."

"Her pack." Edgar eased into the chair in front of the desk. "She's a wolf."

"She's Ruby." Carter sighed as a weight lifted off his chest. Even if Ruby didn't want anyone to know, Carter had no doubts she'd already told Natalia. And Carter needed his brother's advice. Edgar knew how to keep a secret. He was practically a walking cipher himself. He held his cards so close to his chest, even his brothers knew nothing about his social life – if he had one — or his plans or hopes or fears. Carter dared a glance at Edgar. "Don't tell anyone."

"Ruby O'Shea?" Edgar's eyebrows climbed to his hairline, and he laced his hands behind his head. "Your mate is Ruby O'Shea?"

"Yeah." Carter returned his attention to the window and the city beyond. It always looked so damn peaceful from the thirtieth floor – people scurrying around like ants, and cars veering back and forth like little toys. "She can barely conceptualize taking a mate because it threatens what she's built with Rafe, or so she thinks. So most of her heart is already dedicated to being alpha of her pack. There's not much left over."

Edgar made a thoughtful noise. "So she's trying to get you out of her system, and then back to business as usual?"

"I suppose." Carter attempted a smile and swiveled in the chair to square up to the desk. Ready for work, and numbers, and anything to take his mind off the thought of covering Ruby in chocolate syrup and bacon. "I'm working on it. She'll come to her senses."

"Don't give up, Carter." Edgar pushed to his feet, shaking his head. "If she's your mate, she's your mate. Move the world to show her what that means. Do what you have to do. I don't want to see you miserable the rest of your life because your mate lives with her brother a couple blocks away and you still see her every day but can't have her."

"I know, Ed. Go help Logan figure out how to send flowers." Carter waited until the door shut behind his older brother before he leaned back in the chair and covered his face to stifle a groan. No doubt whatever Evershaw was up to had something to do with the offer he'd made Ruby — or with her rejection. He needed to warn her, and soon.

chapter 11

My legs were still a little shaky as I met Natalia at a wedding gown designer, downtown. Luckily it wasn't too far from my apartment, and even though I couldn't straddle my motorcycle without wincing, I gritted it out until I reached the showroom. I groaned as I pulled off my helmet and massaged my lower back, glancing around the neighborhood to gauge whether I should call Rafe to let him know where I was. Some of the recent issues with Evershaw left questions about how far he would go to consolidate power around himself, and I wouldn't put it past him to ambush me in broad daylight.

I walked into the designer's showroom and headed for the back, taking a glass of champagne offered by one of the assistants, and found Natalia already in a half-finished dress, standing on a small dais surrounded by mirrors. She saw me approach in the reflection and smiled. "Hey. Glad you made it."

"Cheers." I raised the glass of champagne and flopped onto a comfortable chaise nearby. "You look lovely, by the way."

She made a face in the mirror and finally faced me, looking down at the wide ball gown skirt that flared around her. "Thanks. I wasn't sure about it. Everyone says you know the dress when you find it, but I didn't. I like it enough, though."

"Kind of like Logan?" I grinned to show her I was only joking, but she still gave me an arch look.

Nat frowned at her cleavage, fussing with the neckline. "I swear, my tits are getting bigger every day. At this rate I'm going to have basketballs stuffed in the front of this dress."

"I'm sure Logan won't mind." I sank lower on the chaise to ease the ache in my core, and rested my head on the back. A nap might be in order, so long as Carter wasn't there to keep me awake. "But it'll be hell on your tailoring bill."

"Like I have a tailoring bill," she said under her breath. Natalia eyed me critically. "What's up with you?"

"I'm just tired." I forced myself to sit up.

"Don't bullshit me, girl." She stepped off the dais and a shower of pins fell to the floor, along with half her dress. Nat cursed and a bevy of assistants fluttered up to disassemble the dress and gather the loose pins. Nat covered her face until they were gone, then leveled a look at me. "Seriously. What's up?"

I waited until everyone else left the room before I rubbed my temples. "I may have slept with Carter."

"*What*?" Natalia said, wearing only some really expensive but really slutty lingerie, practically fell off the dais to sit on the chaise next to me. "When? Why? How?"

"We went to dinner last night." I tried not to laugh, wondering if her shock was due to my getting laid or who I'd slept with. "He looked at some of the records from the bar, and..."

I trailed off with a shrug, and she smacked her forehead. "And you fell into bed with him?"

"He can be very charming."

"I know." Natalia leaned back to study me. "I'm torn. Normally I would ask for details but Carter's like my little brother. I save beaters for him to lick when I make frosting, for God's sake. So I don't think I want to know details, but you can tell me if you had a good time."

And she braced herself, as if preparing to hear that Carter was good in bed.

I laughed and levered to my feet. "I'm not going to tell you anything." But I exaggerated a limp as I retrieved my maid of honor dress from the other side of the room and she made a pained sound, somewhere between a gargle and a groan. Natalia fell sideways across the chaise and I snickered, even though it made my stomach hurt. I stripped off my shirt so I could try on the damn dress. "I'm kidding, I'm kidding. Just…totally vanilla. Nothing exciting. Barely worth mentioning."

She made another strangled sound, and I glanced back. "What?"

"Clearly it was vanilla," she said, still sounding like she wanted to vomit. "By the bite marks and handprints all over your body."

Shit. I looked in the mirror over my shoulder and caught sight of a vast array of bruises, and bites, and little red marks that could have been from anything we'd done. "Well..." I couldn't come up with an intelligent end to that sentence, and instead just stripped off my jeans. "If those bother you, don't look at my ass. I'm pretty sure he left a face-print on my lady business, too, so..."

She howled and threw a pillow at me. "Oh my God, seriously. I already have morning sickness, I do not need to know that Carter spent most of the night fucking you."

"And most of the morning." I stepped into the dress but got a good look at her face in the mirror. I dared a glance back to wink at her. "We did it in my kitchen. I came there before I came here."

Nat muttered, "I hate you so much right now," and then stepped onto the dais behind me to zip up the dress. "But you look beautiful."

"Thanks." I frowned as I turned in the mirror, uncertain whether the black drop-waist gown flattered or just made me look hippy. The deep cleavage and open back put some of Carter's handiwork on display, though most of it seemed to be healing. Not quickly enough, by the look on Nat's face. "I don't think it'll work, though."

"Why not?" She made a face and tugged at where the material bunched at my waist. "Just make sure you're not all bruised and bitten the night of the party, okay? I don't want to think of Carter nibbling on you every time I look at the pictures."

"He's too nice." I sighed as she gave me a sharp look, but we both clamped our mouths shut as the designer and the assistants returned to work on my gown. By the time they'd pinned and measured and tucked the fabric around me, Natalia looked ready to explode from not talking. The other women retreated, taking the gown with them with only a few raised eyebrows at my extracurricular activities, and as I got dressed again I held up a hand to fend her off. "And don't say anything nice. Seriously. I'm an alpha and I need a badass mate. Or none at all."

"Says who?" She arched an eyebrow and buttoned up her shirt. "Who says what you need or must have? I thought you were the alpha and you made your own damn rules."

"It's just reality, Nat." I rubbed my shoulder and searched for my boots. "Okay? I can't face down Miles Evershaw and Barrett Kaiser and Harrison Armstrong and...your Logan with a weak mate. I can't. It's just how it is."

"Oh, so Logan's power and standing is diminished because I'm human, and weak? The other alphas look down on him because he chose me?" Her expression darkened, and a hard glint turned her eyes angry.

I held up my hands, fussing with my ponytail as her face reddened and she looked ready to brawl. "No. Because he's male, they don't judge him."

"And because you're not, suddenly you're held to higher standards?"

"Aren't *you*?" The words burst out before I could take them back. I shoved my foot into a boot and nearly twisted my ankle, but stomped my feet just to make the point. "Jesus Christ, Nat, don't you have to be twice the chef any male chef is, just to get in the room? Don't you have to prove yourself, over and over, just to stay part of the conversation? It's a thousand times harder for me to maintain my position because I know, every time I walk into a room, every male there is wondering whether he could beat me. I'm twice the fighter Rafe is. I can beat him up and down this room without breaking a sweat, but he's in half as many rank fights as I get. No one challenges him, because he *looks* like an alpha. He's what they expect. But me — they think they can beat me because I'm female, so I have to fight twice as hard."

I turned away as frustration made the words stick in my throat. I always thought she understood, that she above all would know what it meant for me to surrender some control to a man, for me to be vulnerable enough to care about someone. "They're going to judge me by who stands next to me, Nat, and that person could literally dismantle what I've spent the last ten years building."

"If that's what happens, it wasn't worth keeping to start with."

I turned to confront her, ready to fight, and found her with her arms folded over her chest and a fierce expression. She set me back on my heels, and Natalia jabbed a finger in my sternum as she stepped forward. "Look, you. This isn't you. The Ruby I know doesn't give a fuck what everyone else thinks, and she sure as hell doesn't give a fuck what Miles fucking Evershaw thinks. Are you *kidding* me? If those stupid jackasses judge you because you love Carter and want him in your life, then that's their problem. There is absolutely nothing in the world that they could do to shake your pack's faith in you, or turn your pack against you. And if somehow, in some ridiculous twist of fate, Carter is the reason that the pack kicks you out – fuck them, too. Carter would help you make a new pack, a better pack, and you'd better damn well believe that Logan and I, and the rest of the family, will be there to help."

Breathing hard, she scowled at me and started to poke me again. I dodged and stayed out of her reach. "Jesus, Nat. Breathe."

"Don't make me mad, Ruby Leigh O'Shea." Her cheeks flushed. "I hate seeing you like this. I don't know if this is something to do with Carter, or Evershaw, or what, but this isn't you. Hike up your big girl panties. *You* are the alpha. You could pick a human bum for your mate, and if that's who you're supposed to be with — that's who you're going to be with. If one of those men says a damn word to you about it, then we will both show them why it's a terrible idea to judge someone over love. Got it?"

"Yeah, I've got it." I caught her shoulders and steered her toward the chaise. "Just…calm down. You look like your face is going to explode."

"I don't like seeing you so uncertain." She touched her stomach and reached for a bottle of water, cooling next to the bottle of champagne. "If you start getting all wishy-washy, the whole damn city might be coming down around my ears."

I sat on the dais to study her, though I tried to hide it as I fussed with my boots. "Did you really have to use my middle name?"

She shot me a sideways look. "You were being ridiculous. That was the only way to get your attention."

"Thanks." I snorted, shaking my head. "But I still don't know if it'll work with Carter."

I barely dodged the bottle of water as it sailed past my head, and Natalia threw her hands in the air in exasperation. "You have *got* to be…"

"Excuse me, Ms. Spencer?" The designer poked her head in from the main showroom. "There is a delivery for you."

"A delivery?" Natalia sat up, double-checked that her clothes were all done up, double-checked me, then nodded to the woman. "Thank you, please let them in."

"You are a lucky woman," she said, then stood out of the way as a white-suited deliveryman strode in carrying two enormous bouquets of gorgeous stargazer lilies and purple larkspur.

Natalia blinked as he handed her one, then turned to offer the second to me. I took it, at a loss for what else to do, then sneezed. A second man appeared to hand over two boxes wrapped beautifully in clean white paper, with a ribbon curled in a bow on top. He smiled and clicked his heels together as he gestured at the box Natalia held. "Fresh saltwater taffy for Ms. Spencer, and fresh caramels for Ms. O'Shea. Please, enjoy."

When the door shut behind them both and we were alone, I looked at Natalia with my eyebrows raised in question. What the hell? She shook her head, fishing around in the flowers for a card. She flipped it open with a frown, read for a moment, then started laughing. She held up a very small tomato, nestled among the larkspur, and tossed it to me. "I had a moment this morning and called Logan in tears over some shitty produce. He claims he felt bad I had to face bruised tomatoes, but I see Edgar's fingerprints all over this. The candy is definitely Edgar."

"Why the hell did *I* get flowers and candy?" My mouth watered at the thought of fresh caramel, though. The box still felt warm. Natalia, at least, wouldn't judge me if I broke it open and devoured every one.

"Because you're here and you're awesome." She inhaled from the lilies and smiled, brushing the petals with her fingertips. "And maybe it was Carter's idea."

My cheeks burned. "He shouldn't be sending me flowers. That's not part of our agreement."

"Then see if you have a note, idiot."

I fished through the leaves, still tempted by the caramel, and found a small white card hidden among the flowers. '*Thank you for a wonderful evening*' was printed on it, but that was it. I frowned, flipping it over, but found nothing else. It seemed unlike Carter, but oh well. They were beautiful flowers.

Natalia broke open the taffy and papers rustled as she fished for a specific flavor. "Are you hungry? We should get lunch. I'm not sure where to put the flowers, but we'll find a place. Come back to the house with me and we'll figure this all out."

It was tempting. Hanging out at the mansion usually meant Natalia would cook, and I would stay for dinner, which meant Logan's amazing wine cellar, and probably a movie in their private theater, and staying over in a gorgeous spa-like guest room. A girl could get used to that kind of luxury. But I shook my head, gathering up the flowers and candy. "I've got to be at the bar tonight, and if I go to the mansion, I won't want to leave."

"The apartment, girl. We can go to the apartment." Nat heaved to her feet with an unladylike grunt, and took one more look at the white wedding dress hanging on a stand. "But whatever I make for lunch should be low cal. Definitely."

"I don't think you know how to cook anything without a pound of butter," I said under my breath, and she gave me a dirty look. I helped her juggle the flowers and candy and bag, sneezing again as leaves tickled my nose. "But I'll help you get this stuff back to the apartment. I forgot you and Logan found a place close by."

"Very convenient." She glanced at me sideways but paused to thank the designer, kiss her on both cheeks, and wave to the flock of assistants. When we were outside, Natalia fished around in her bag and offered me a key. "So if you ever need to use it for anything, feel free."

"I'm not using your love nest with Logan as a place to take Carter." I flushed at the thought. We'd have to clean every inch of it just to make sure Logan didn't know by smell that we'd been there.

Natalia snorted and shoved the key into my bag. "Please. It's nicer than your place by a mile. Just call ahead to make sure we're not using it. If Edgar has a late meeting, sometimes he'll stay there, as well. There are two spare bedrooms. Help yourself to either one. And give me a head's up so I can send the maid over."

I chewed my lower lip as I loaded the flowers in the backseat of her expensive sedan, outfitted with every security feature imaginable. "I don't think I'll ever use it. But thank you for the key."

"You're welcome." She braced her hands on her lower back and stretched, making a face. "Ugh. Trying on dresses is rough this early in the morning. I could use a nap and a sandwich. Let's go."

"I'll follow you on the bike," I said, and tilted my head at where the motorcycle waited.

"Suit yourself." She slid into the driver's seat but rolled down the window as she held up the white box of caramel. "But your candy might not survive the four blocks to the apartment."

I leaned in to take it back, laughing. "I will cut a bitch over some caramel, Nat."

She laughed as she drove off, and I took an extra minute to secure the box to the back of the motorcycle. I dialed Carter's number on my phone, but I hesitated before I hit send. I finally hit the button before I chickened out, and I almost hung up five different times as it rang and rang.

But Carter's voice, smooth as caramel, made my knees knock and heat rush through me when he answered. "Hey there. This is a nice surprise."

"I wanted to thank you for the flowers." I didn't sound particularly grateful, though. I pinched the bridge of my nose and stared down at the sidewalk under my boots. "I mean, thank you for the flowers and the candy. They're lovely. Very thoughtful."

A slight pause ignited doubt in my chest, and for a second I thought I'd made a terrible mistake. Then he chuckled and said, "You're very welcome. Did you and Natalia have a good morning?"

"Trying on dresses is never fun," I said, chewing my lip as I looked around the street. Jesus. I felt like a damn teenager sneaking calls to her boyfriend after curfew, trying not to wake my parents. "But the flowers saved the day."

"I'm glad. What are you doing for dinner tonight?"

"I have to keep an eye on the bar tonight." I picked at a thread on my jeans, feeling a little queasy and nervous and excited, all at the same time. "So that's where I'll be from two this afternoon until probably three in the morning. Later, if there's anything to clean up."

"Good. I'll know where to find you." Someone else spoke in the background and he grumbled something at them, then dropped his voice as he went on. "I'll stop by the bar, then. See you tonight."

I opened my mouth to ask whether that meant business or a date, but he'd already hung up. I growled in frustration as I shoved the phone in my pocket and kicked the bike to life before heading toward Nat's apartment. I didn't like surprises very much, and Carter Chase was the biggest surprise of all.

chapter 12

Sitting at his desk for the rest of the afternoon seemed more tortuous than normal. He barely made it through lunch with Edgar and Benedict before Edgar told him to go check on business at Natalia's restaurant. He was in the back office at the restaurant when Ruby called, and her husky voice sent shivers all the way through him. He also felt like a kid, hiding in the storeroom so no one would overhear, in case he sounded like a love-struck idiot. And then the anticipation of seeing her that evening, being with her in public, distracted him for the rest of the day.

He remembered to call Edgar to verify whether his older brother was behind the flowers and candy, and Edgar just laughed. Apparently Logan failed at figuring out how to send flowers, so Edgar took over and added a bit just to complicate Carter's life as well. But Carter knew he owed Edgar one.

Carter managed to put together a few recommendations for Ruby's business plan, and changed into jeans and a sweater at the office before heading to the bar around seven. They all kept wardrobes at every possible place they would stop in the city, mostly because shifting ruined a lot of clothes. And with the long hours at the office when the business world woke up in Tokyo and London, variety in clothing choices made all the difference. So he was at least wearing comfortable clothes as he drove to O'Shea's.

When he walked in, Ruby stood behind the bar, leaning on her elbows as she talked to some strange dude. The lion immediately wanted to kill the guy. Or at least roar enough to scare him off. But Carter only gripped the business portfolio containing his notes until his nails punched through the leather. Rafe waved at him but Carter barely noticed, making a beeline to the bar.

She straightened as he approached, and a smile slid across her face. It made him think of breakfast in her kitchen. Syrup. They could try syrup next time. Get sticky in all the right places. Ruby's head tilted and her cheeks grew pink. Maybe she could read his mind.

Carter took a stool farther down the bar, nodding at her. "Beer, if you don't mind."

"Sure." She pulled a pint glass, but gave him an odd look. "Why are you all scowly?"

He frowned, about to argue, but she put a coaster on the bar, tossed salt across it, and put the beer in front of him. Her eyes sparked gold, and her head tilted just slightly enough to indicate the skinny dude at the other end of the bar. "Don't tell me it was our friend the jackal?"

Carter concentrated on the beer, draining the pint glass before setting the empty in front of her. "Of course not. One more, please."

Half her mouth curled in a smile. "Come on, Chase. Admit it. You're jealous."

He killed the second beer before he opened the portfolio, but kept his voice low, in case the jackal had prying ears. "Why would I be jealous? It's not like you're mine."

Something changed in her expression, as if he'd rejected her, and Ruby started wiping down the bar a few feet away. "Right. I'm not."

Carter leaned over the bar to grab her wrist, drawing her closer, close enough he could breathe, "If you were, yes. I would be jealous. I would rip that guy's fucking throat out, because he was staring down your shirt and probably thinking unclean thoughts."

He met her gaze long enough for her to see the lion peering out, for her to hear the growl that rumbled from the animal side of him, and when her lips parted and her cheeks flushed, he released her. Sat back on the stool and sipped his third beer. He glanced at her as Ruby rubbed her arm and set out a bowl of popcorn at his elbow. Carter said, "You guys ready to talk business?"

"This is a business meeting?" He thought he saw disappointment in her eyes, but couldn't be sure. Ruby shrugged. "Sure."

She called Rafe over, and he shook Carter's hand with a smile. "Good to see you, man. Heard you're working out with Kaiser's guys these days. Expecting some fights in the near future?"

"Maybe." Carter tried not to think of Ruby, of fighting for Ruby. He'd get in the ring for her. He'd face down the bears or her entire pack, if that's what it took. "Mostly, it's good business sense. The bears want to train some MMA fighters, try to get someone on the circuit. It's a good investment. If you have some extra cash lying around, you might want to point it toward Kaiser."

"No extra cash, friend." Rafe grimaced, his dark eyebrows heavy enough to nearly conceal his eyes. "Ruby said you were looking into some other business planning for us?"

"Yep." Carter opened the folio and handed them a couple of proposals. Somehow it was easier, less disconcerting, to address Rafe more than Ruby. At least Rafe couldn't set his heart racing, or make his lion purr with just a look. Carter cleared his throat. "Here's the thing. O'Shea's appeals to a certain clientele. You've designed it for yourselves and your friends, but that doesn't necessarily draw in the money. If you want to expand, you're going to have to appeal to a larger demographic."

Ruby got a guarded look on her face, watching him even though she held up the papers to read. "What kind of demographic?"

"People with money." Rafe snorted, shaking his head, and looked around the bar. "This is a dive, Carter. It's always been a dive. We like it that way."

"Exactly. If it's a dive, you're not going to get the traffic you need to increase revenue. Without increased revenue, you can't expand to other locations or enterprises. Ruby said you didn't want to take on a bank loan or other investors. If that's not the case, let me know because that changes our calculus considerably. If that is the case, well. Your options are limited to making changes here."

Ruby eyed him as she refilled his beer yet again, and Carter wondered for a split second if she wanted to get him drunk. Her septum piercing flashed as she leaned on the bar, giving him a peek at her generous cleavage. "Like what kinds of changes?"

He refused to look anywhere but her face, though the effort not to stare at her breasts probably took a year off his life. "Get a better chef to start, and expand the menu. Consider lunch and dinner hours and specials, as well as happy hour and after hours deals. Book live music as many nights as you can. Expand your beer selection, run some cocktail specials. Advertise more. Fancy up the décor, and replace some of the broken chairs. Move the pool table so you've got more room for tables and a dance floor."

"You trying to class this place up, Chase?" Rafe rubbed the back of his neck, already shaking his head. "That's not us. The O'Shea's are not classy. BloodMoon is a tough pack, not some fancy ass lion pride like you and your brothers. Blue collar."

"That's where we started," Ruby said under her breath, elbowing her brother. "That's not where we want to stay. Right?"

"Yeah, but come on. Bee, we won't even recognize this place if we change it that much."

Bee? Carter bit back a smile as Ruby gave him a sharp look, and he knew Rafe would get an earful for letting that cute nickname into the wild. Carter wanted to call her Bee. Make her buzz a little. He snorted to himself, and stared into his beer glass. Best not let that show on his face.

"That's the point," she said, tone dry. The bar towel swiped dangerously close to his glass and Carter bit the inside of his cheek. Ruby gestured at the rest of the bar. "If we want to make more, we have to do more, Rafe."

"Let's start with the kitchen," he said. "The menu can definitely use some improvement."

"What I would recommend," Carter said, tapping the bar near the other man's elbow. "Is to do it all and have a grand re-opening. Advertise across the city. Maybe run a special with Nat's restaurant – they have dinner at her place, then a free drink at yours. Start fresh without some of the old baggage."

"We don't have baggage." Rafe sounded indignant, sitting up and squaring his shoulders.

"We have a little baggage," Ruby said, and once again Carter snorted. She scowled and reached over the bar to poke him in the chest. "Quiet in the peanut gallery, Chase."

He held up his hands. "I'm just a disinterested third party. Unless you want me to be more."

She froze, eyes wide, a panicked look on her face. Like he would propose to her in the middle of her bar, and right in front of her brother. Carter wanted to laugh so badly, he had to gouge his thumbnail into his leg to keep a straight face. Rafe remained oblivious, shuffling through the papers. "What, you want to invest or something?"

"That would be part of it." He let the silence hang, just to torment Ruby a little more, then handed them the second business proposal. "And I would be your business manager, as well. I have some personal funds I would like to invest, and if you're willing to make some changes to the bar and follow these recommendations, I'd be happy to be your business partner."

Rafe grunted, scanning the new paperwork, and Ruby gave Carter the most evil look he could remember receiving. And he'd almost been paralyzed by Benedict's half-Medusa mate, Eloise. Turned out, she had some competition when Ruby got mad. Carter rubbed his mouth to hide the rest of his smile, not wanting to antagonize her any further. "Read it over, think it over, let me know. A grand re-opening ahead of the holidays would be best, so we'd need to get moving if you're interested in what I've proposed."

"Funny how you're going around proposing things," Ruby said, moving down the bar to pull pints for a couple of other customers. When she finished, she tossed the towel across her shoulder and eyed Carter askance. "I told you we didn't want to take out a loan."

"This isn't a loan." Carter half-turned on the stool as a commotion grew around the door, and a few newcomers entered the bar with a blast of cold air. "It's an investment."

Rafe's attention shifted to the newcomers as they hustled up the bar, and a frown drew down his substantial eyebrows. "What's going on?"

The skinny kid eyed Carter but answered the wolf alpha without hesitation. "Just heard something from one of Evershaw's guys."

Ruby went still, a gold sheen washing over her eyes.

The kid's throat bobbed as he gulped under the full weight of alpha attention. "SilverLine plans to petition the Council to mandate only one wolf pack in the city. All other packs would have to live outside the city limits, or petition Evershaw to remain in his territory."

A strangled noise escaped from Ruby, and her features twisted as she bared her teeth. "He *what*?"

The kid cowered and shuffled a little to half-hide behind Carter, talking faster. "He's already contacted some members of the Council and requested an emergency session. Evershaw claims it will help clarify territory and maintain order. He wants to implement it immediately."

"That son of a bitch," Rafe said. The white edges of his teeth showed as he stared across the bar with a distant look, his hands clenched into fists. Then his gold gaze shifted to Carter. "Did you hear about this?"

"Evershaw didn't call us." Carter refused to cower or look away from the thunder brewing in Rafe's expression, or the lightning already sparking from Ruby. "We heard from the bears this morning that Evershaw called around to all the alphas to request the emergency session."

"You didn't tell me," Ruby said. As if Carter betrayed her.

Carter took a deep breath, shaking his head. "Edgar was working on more details. There wasn't much to say."

Rafe growled and smashed his fist on the bar. "I'll fucking kill Evershaw. We've been here longer than he has, the piece of shit."

Ruby looked at the messenger kid and said, "You can go." She waited until he retreated, every line in the kid's body radiating relief, then leaned closer to her brother. "And you're not going to fight Evershaw. I am."

Carter wanted to lurch forward, grab her, and drag her away to the mansion until she forgot about having anything to do with Miles Evershaw. He stared at the polished surface of the bar until he thought for sure smoke wisped out of it, but couldn't look at Ruby. He wasn't going to interfere. This was just part of her role as alpha. As much as the idea of her fighting anyone made his skin crawl and his lion roar, he had to keep his cool.

Rafe shook his head immediately. "No way. No way in hell."

"Evershaw can beat you." Ruby shot Carter a warning look and returned to the nearly-inaudible conference with her brother. "And we both know it. No ego, Rafe. I can beat Evershaw. I can. And he knows it."

"There's no way he'll face you in the ring to decide this."

Ruby shook her head, arms crossed. "He'll have to. We're both alpha. We decide who fights. If we decide I fight him, then I fight him."

"What if he refuses?" Rafe still looked on the verge of a shift, ready to run into the night to hunt down Miles Evershaw. "He'll claim he won't fight a woman. You know he will."

"We'll tell the Council he forfeits. If they want to go forward with this stupidity, they can't dictate all the rules."

Carter dug his fingers into his arm to keep from tackling her to protect her from even the implied threat of the other wolf pack. Maybe Logan could have a word with Evershaw and impress upon the asshole why games like these were the whole reason the Council existed. Every shifter in the city had enough of bullshit rank games. There was no reason two or even three wolf packs couldn't exist within the city limits. Except when one had an asshole for an alpha.

Rafe rubbed his jaw. "I don't like it, Bee. Especially with…what else he talked about earlier. What if this is just a ploy to get you to agree to that?"

"I will never mate with Evershaw," Ruby said, enunciating every syllable. "Ever. If this is some lame attempt to get my attention, then great. He's got my attention, and it's not the good kind. We are not running away from this."

"Of course we aren't." Rafe grumbled, then shot Carter a dark look. "Can we expect the Pride's support?"

"I can only speak for myself," Carter said. He hated to play the politics, and while he couldn't imagine Logan ever voting against the O'Shea pack in favor of Evershaw, he couldn't speak for Logan. "But of course I'm with your pack. And with how Natalia feels about Ruby, I'm guessing Logan will also side with you if he values his life."

Rafe snorted, then shoved to his feet. "I need to go for a run. Are you good to run the place tonight, Bee?"

"Yeah. Get out of here before I kill you for calling me 'Bee.'" Ruby threw the dirty towel at him.

Rafe strode to the back office and disappeared, leaving Ruby to eye Carter. He tried to look relaxed and calm, not as though his guts seethed with the desperate need to protect her. Ruby handed him another beer, her eyebrow arched. "You okay over there, Chase?"

"I've been better, Bee."

A hint of a smile touched her face and disappeared. "Then why have you gouged my bar?"

Carter looked down to see where his nails created rents in the smooth wood, and cleared his throat as he gingerly picked up the beer instead. "Because sometimes that's the only thing that keeps the lion inside, particularly when someone important is threatened."

She picked up another bar towel and snapped it in his direction. "Watch yourself. But good job. I didn't think you'd make it through that conversation."

"I'm serious." Carter shrugged and focused on the beer. "It's pack business, it's your business. As much as I would like to find Miles Evershaw, rip his heart out, and throw him into a wood-chipper feet-first, I acknowledge that type of reaction is not helpful for your pack relationships."

Ruby laughed. "Good job. You hungry?"

"I already ate." And the beer filled him up as well, the dark beer that was practically a meal in and of itself. "But thank you."

She leaned on the bar under the guise of examining the scratches, and her breath warmed his cheek as she murmured, "If you want to stick around, we can head back to my place after last call?"

"Sure." Carter concentrated on gathering his papers and putting them back in the folio. "I'll work on my homework."

Another smile flashed before she put on her serious face and handed him a towel. "Or I'll put you to work back here. Can you pull pints?"

He pushed to his feet, the lion content because he would be close to their mate, and slid around her into the narrow space behind the massive wooden bar. "I can do anything you need me to do."

"Don't let your mouth write checks your ass can't cash," she said under her breath, and he laughed.

He cracked his knuckles and started lining up pint glasses. She had no idea how much her mouth owed him, and he meant to collect.

chapter 13

By last call every one of my muscles ached, my knees hurt, my back hurt, and a headache pounded behind my eyes from the cigarette smoke and music and shouting and trying to convince my wolf not to fuck Carter right there behind the bar. He drove me home and even opened my door, and everything was warm and dizzy and perfect. Comforting. I liked having him in my den. I liked coming home to his scent on my pillows and in my kitchen.

Carter arched an eyebrow at me. "You look exhausted."

"I am exhausted." I tried to laugh as I rubbed my temples. "Sorry. I thought I would be more fun."

"More fun?" His purr rumbled in his chest and he eased closer to slide his arms around me and draw me into a tight hug. "This is fun. But there's something else I had in mind."

My stomach tightened at the thought of another night of marathon sex, but I had to be up early to meet Natalia and then start lining up interviews for a new chef. When I hesitated, Carter chuckled. He rubbed his cheek against my head and patted me gently on the butt before he turned me toward the bedroom and gave me a little push. "Go put on your robe while I get your surprise ready."

"Do I need to take some aspirin before we get started?"

"It probably wouldn't hurt." He winked as he said it, so I wasn't entirely sure whether I should believe him. But I took a handful of painkillers anyway as he headed into the bathroom and I retreated to the bedroom.

By the time I stripped off my clothes and wore only my ratty old bathrobe, the apartment was quiet once more. And dark. I frowned as I stepped into the hell, then blinked as Carter stuck his head out of the bathroom. "Are you ready?"

"Yes," I said, though a little warily. No telling what kind of surprise the lion had in store for me.

From his expression, he knew perfectly well what I was thinking. His cheek dimpled as he grinned. And then he led me into the bathroom, lit only by candles, where the tub was filled with bubbles and water and a few rose petals. I blinked. Blinked again. But no, my eyes remained blurry and then overflowed. A hot bath. Seriously.

He chuckled and rubbed my back, not commenting as I dashed the tears off my cheeks, and he helped me take off the robe. It didn't escape my notice that he wore only a towel, and that did nothing at all to hide how excited he was to see me. Carter eased into the water first, settling into the wide tub, and I stepped in after him to sit between his legs. I almost moaned as the hot water surrounded me, rushed to relax all the tension and anger from my muscles.

Carter made the grumbly noise that got my wolf all excited, and his thighs tightened around my hips as he rubbed my shoulders. "Relax, baby."

I let my head fall back against his shoulder as Carter continued to knead the tension out of my muscles, down my arms, across my lower back. His magic hands turned me boneless and weightless in a couple of minutes, and the soft scent of lavender and honeysuckle did the rest. He lathered body wash between his hands and began to wash every inch of me. With particular attention to a few specific areas. I floated, feeling sleek and smooth and pampered, as his fingers dipped between my legs.

Carter kissed the side of my neck as his knee lifted and eased my leg open a little more. With the rush of hot water against my slit came more heat and his skillful hands. There was no rush to his efforts. He didn't want to finish me off just so he could fuck me. It felt caring and simple — a lion taking care of his mate. Loving her.

My hips moved to meet his hand as his thumb pressed against my clit and his fingers slid inside me, and I gripped his wrist in desperation. His free hand squeezed my breast and I moaned, undulating until water splashed out of the tub and my head tossed on his shoulder. I rode the wave of passion, eyes half-closed, as Carter continued to move his fingers through the clenching muscles at my core. When I finally relaxed against him, no longer frozen in ecstasy,

Carter smoothed my hair out of his face and kissed my shoulder.

His voice was husky and deep. "There. That's better."

I sighed and managed to lift one arm to rub the back of his neck. "Good job, Chase."

"Be careful with all that sweet talk or I'll start to think you've gone soft."

It made me smile, but I still couldn't open my eyes. I felt languid and slow, perfectly content to float there in the bathtub as aftershocks trembled through me. "I'll keep that in mind."

Carter kissed behind my ear and down my shoulder, his palm flat on my stomach. "I want to get you a nicer den."

"Hmm?" I could hardly keep myself awake with the warmth of his body and the water all around.

"You need a better apartment." His arm tightened around me briefly, as if to reassure himself I was still there, then he adjusted his legs. "A nicer apartment, bigger. In a better part of town."

I forced my eyes open. "Why?"

"Because this neighborhood isn't safe." Carter yawned. "And for me to do half the things I want to do to you, we need more room."

"We'll see," I managed to say. "At the end of two weeks. Right?"

He made an irritated noise. "Then I'll rent an apartment and you can stay with me."

I closed my eyes again and reached up to pat his cheek. "We're not arguing about this in a bathtub, Chase."

He didn't speak but it wasn't quite as comfortable a silence as before. I took a deep breath before I maneuvered a little in the water and managed to get his hard cock standing up between my legs instead of digging into my back. "I was proud of how you handled yourself today, at the bar. You could have said something to Rafe, and you didn't. Thank you."

"You're welcome," he said, though his voice sounded odd.

I wiggled in his lap and watched the pink head of his cock appear next to my clit before I lifted and it slid back once more. Carter held my waist tightly, lifting me up, and I reached down to stroke his cock before positioning the head against the slippery flesh at my entrance. He said something under his breath that I couldn't hear or understand as he thrust up and pulled me down, and he filled me. I gripped the side of the tub as I moved and he moved and water splashed everywhere. Carter held me tightly as his hips jerked up and up and up, and his hand pressed once more between my legs to find my clit. I cried out and writhed in his grip as he grunted and came in a sudden rush, sinking his teeth in to my shoulder. Stars dotted my vision and my breathing grew ragged as I collapsed back against him.

Carter took a moment to catch his breath, then he kissed my shoulder and stood me up. "I'm too old to fuck in a bathtub, I'll be black and blue for weeks. Get your ass to the bed."

I didn't immediately follow directions but instead turned and hugged him, letting my head rest against his chest so I could hear the comforting thump of his heartbeat. I closed my eyes and reveled in the security of his arms. "Thank you for the bath, Carter."

He squeezed me tight and kissed the top of my head. "You're welcome, Bee."

As I gingerly stepped onto the tile floor and the small lake of bath water we'd splashed out, he snapped a hand towel at my butt and arched his eyebrows. "You've got to the count of three."

I didn't make it, maybe a little bit on purpose.

chapter 14

Carter concentrated on hitting the heavy bag with all his strength. He'd slacked off on his workouts in the past week, too consumed with Ruby to do much other than work and fuck. She'd even called him in the middle of the afternoon, and he met her at her apartment without blinking. He missed a meeting with Logan and some investors, and it didn't even occur to him to check his schedule. As soon as he heard her voice, he was hooked. He knew he was addicted to her – touching her, tasting her, smelling her. Waking up with her all naked and warm, pressed against him.

He shook the thought from his head and kneed the bag. Every moment he spent with her just made it that much more difficult to face the possibility of losing her. If she decided to walk away, to choose her pack over him, he might lose his mind. The lion sure as hell would. Edgar would have to lock him up in a cage for the next year to keep him from going after Ruby. Maybe the rest of his life.

Carter stepped back, wiping some of the sweat from his face, and jumped as someone said, "Did that bag in particular say something to offend you, or do you just hate all red bags?"

He turned and saw Eloise watching him with a raised eyebrow. Carter sighed. "Got a lot on my mind. What's up?"

Benedict's girlfriend worked as a receptionist at the gym, partly because she needed a job, but mostly because she was part Medusa and could paralyze any shifters who got out of control. The bears took safety seriously, and Eloise's very presence kept things under control. Apparently, she'd done security for the illegal street-fights run by the coyotes, and her reputation preceded her. So the uncertainty in her expression worried him. A lot.

"Well." Eloise played with her phone, gray-silver eyes sliding away from his as her dark hair snuck over her shoulder in a clingy rope. "Todd Evershaw called."

Carter snorted and turned away. "Girl, don't tell Benedict that."

She followed him, making a face, but caught his sleeve to pull him up short. "What am I, stupid? Of course I'm not going to tell him. Besides, he's in a big business meeting thing all afternoon, and I couldn't reach him anyway."

Carter studied her through narrowed eyes, a hint of unease uncoiling in his stomach. Eloise's normally unflappable demeanor, honed through years of criminal work, had entirely disappeared. She looked nervous. "What did Todd want?"

"Here's the thing."

"Jesus. There's a thing?" Carter shook his head and went to sit on a nearby bench, pounding a bottle of water before mopping his face with the towel. "You're killing me, Eloise. Please don't tell me you're breaking up with Benedict for Todd Evershaw. Ben would lose his fucking…"

"Don't be ridiculous." She flicked angrily at her hair as it curled and uncurled in a cloud around her head. "I had to promise Miles Evershaw a favor when he helped me with the hyenas. Todd just called to say Miles is ready to cash in. Today. Like, now."

The uneasy feeling grew. Evershaw had been agitating with the Council, despite that the vote had been put off, and trying to gather support from the coyotes, jackals, and other canines for the past several days. It stressed Ruby out until Carter could hardly distract her from it at all. And for Evershaw to call in a favor from someone he knew was close to Ruby and her pack...he didn't like it.

Carter shook his head. "Don't go."

"I have to." She grimaced, glancing down at her phone. "I gave him my word on the favor, Carter. I have to at least hear him out."

He shoved to his feet and headed for the locker room. "Give me a sec to clean up, and I'll drive you. I know Benedict wouldn't want you going in there alone."

"Thanks, Carter." She chewed her lower lip. "I'm supposed to meet them at his office."

The relief in her tone convinced him he did the right thing, even though his skin crawled with the urge to strangle Miles Evershaw. Walking into the wolf's den already angry meant things would escalate. He took a cold shower to try to work through some of the irritation, and felt more at ease by the time he dressed and met Eloise outside at his car. She still looked nervous, fiddling with her phone, and occasionally trying to control her hair.

It took about twenty minutes to reach the warehouse district where Miles Evershaw kept his offices. Before they got out of the car, Carter took a deep breath. "If anything happens, paralyze whoever's close, and get out of there. I'll buy you as much time as I can. Just don't let them take you hostage, okay? And remember you represent Logan and the rest of the pride. If you start a blood feud, all of us are liable."

"Got it." She stared out the windshield, unmoving, then took a deep breath and calm settled over her.

Carter hadn't seen her go full Medusa since the fight with the hyenas, though Eloise ended up paralyzing herself when the former hyena queen held up a mirror, but even some of the mojo was scary. She turned silver eyes to him and tilted her head at the door. "Ready?"

He got out of the car, going around to open her door, and then they both went to the heavy steel entranceway, where one of Evershaw's cold-faced guards waited. The wolf's lip curled as he looked at Carter. "Only the girl."

Before Carter could do more than growl, Eloise arched an eyebrow and her hair coiled itself into snake-like ropes, arching in a threatening spray around her head. "Try again."

The guy hesitated, taking in the hair and quicksilver eyes, then his radio crackled and he shoved the door open. "Fine. But the lion walks in of his own accord."

"Obviously," she said under her breath, all trace of nerves gone, and practically elbowed the guy out of the way. Carter followed, silent, but kept his attention on high alert as other pack members joined them in the hall.

But at least they gave Eloise plenty of space.

By the time they made it to the back room in the warehouse that served as Miles's office, Carter wanted to jump out of his own skin from feeling stalked, hunted. Those damn wolves on his heels the entire way made his lion prickly. And seeing Miles Evershaw just made Carter want to put his fist through a wall. He imagined the son of a bitch daring to ask Ruby to settle for Miles, because no one else wanted her.

Luckily Carter just had to stand there, arms crossed, as Eloise faced the alpha of SilverLine pack. Todd, Miles's younger brother or cousin or something, hopped up from the couch on the far side of the office and offered the Medusa a charming smile. Apparently the silver eyes and crazy ass hair didn't bother the wolf. "Eloise, lovely to see you again. Do you want a drink?"

"Good to see you, Todd." Her attention returned to his brother, still sitting behind the massive desk. "But I'd rather get this over with. I'd also rather Benedict did not find out about this."

Todd snorted, but he glanced at Carter before he spoke. "The lawyer keeps you on a tight leash, doesn't he?"

"There's a leash involved, but don't assume he's the one holding the business end." She folded her hands at her middle and waited, looking at Miles.

Miles, expressionless as usual, gestured at the chairs in front of his desk. "Sit, please."

"We won't be here long enough for that." Eloise didn't blink.

Carter's irritation with the man grew when he failed to stand up as they entered the room. A typical wolf power play. And downright rude when a woman walked in. His lion snarled and stretched, desperate to show the wolves how dangerous even solitary lions could be.

But the alpha apparently didn't care, because he leaned back in his chair to study them both, and laced his hands behind his head. "You owe me a favor, Eloise. Are you ready to pay up?"

"Yes. And you should recall, Evershaw, that I only agreed to the favor if it would not harm the Chase family or the BloodMoon pack. If you violate either of those conditions, I'm not obligated to agree to pay up."

"I recall." The alpha's eyes darkened, so maybe he'd hoped Eloise had forgotten. Miles pressed his fingers together near his chin and studied her. "The coyotes tell me they owe you a great deal of money, and a couple of favors. They're not in a position to pay you back without destroying their business. So. All I ask of you is to forgive their debt."

"I'm not letting them off the hook for over thirty grand, Evershaw."

The man's eyebrow arched and the lines around his eyes deepened. He looked older, and tired. Distant and adrift. But the moment passed and Miles turned once more into an unfeeling, power-hungry schemer. "If I recall, the favor I provided you saved your life. And I'm sure Benedict would be happy to provide the cash in exchange for...services rendered."

Carter's teeth went on edge. If Eloise went full gorgon on Evershaw, Carter would just let her go. They could deal with the consequences, but Miles had it coming.

Eloise's head tilted as she watched the alpha, her agitated braids the only sign she wasn't having a pleasant conversation about the weather. "What are they giving you in exchange?"

He didn't blink. "That's between me and them."

Carter's heart sank. If Evershaw convinced the coyotes to join the Council under his leadership, chances were the rest of the shifter alphas would allow SilverLine to become the main pack in the city. Which meant Ruby and Rafe would have to obey Evershaw or fight tooth and nail to keep their rank — or find new territory. Outside the city. And Carter would have to follow her or risk his lion plummeting into insanity. He held his breath.

Eloise crossed her arms and narrowed her eyes. "Evershaw, come on. We know what you're up to."

"You owe me a favor." Evershaw leaned forward on his desk, every muscle in his body tense as his gaze hardened. "It's a very simple thing, Eloise – let the coyotes off the hook. That's all I'm asking from you. It has nothing to do with the lions or the O'Sheas."

"But I know perfectly what you're going to..."

"You don't." Evershaw's teeth gleamed as his lip curled in a near-snarl. "You know nothing. If you refuse to fulfill your part of the bargain, Eloise, I'll be forced to file a grievance against you with the Council, and levy an honor debt against you and the rest of your family."

The air crackled around Eloise and her eyes turned liquid as mercury. But her voice came out low and cold and her hair hissed in an angry whisper. "Are you threatening me?"

"It's not a threat if you do what you said you would do."

Carter ground his teeth until his jaw creaked. "Evershaw, this is low, even for you."

The alpha never took his eyes off Eloise. "This doesn't concern you, Chase."

"Bullshit." Carter advanced a step, and Evershaw immediately lurched to his feet.

Eloise grabbed Carter's arm and hauled him back as growling filled the office. She elbowed her way in front of him and jabbed her finger at Evershaw's chest. "You listen to me, Miles Evershaw. Everyone else calls you an asshole, but I didn't believe it until this moment. I know exactly what you plan to do with this favor, and even though you've found a loophole, don't think I will forget this. If any harm befalls BloodMoon or the Chases because of this agreement, I will find you and make you pay."

The dark braids around her head flared out and hissed more, until even Evershaw looked a little nonplussed. Eloise clenched her fists. "The mansion has a very large garden, Evershaw. Someone stole all the garden gnomes. Replacing them with some stone wolves would suit me very nicely."

Todd cleared his throat from the other side of the room, still lounging on the couch as if his brother hadn't almost come to blows with Carter. "Okay, let's all take a deep breath and…"

"Stop." Evershaw didn't blink, but Todd silenced with a click of his teeth. The alpha met Eloise's gaze without breaking a sweat. "Well?"

The medusa gritted her teeth but ground out the words. "Very well. I forgive the debt the coyotes owe me. And I no longer owe you anything."

"Good." Evershaw straightened and turned his attention back to the work on his desk, barely looking at them as he gestured at the door. "Todd will show you out."

Eloise snarled some curses under her breath as she turned to the door, and Carter wondered if she had enough magic to make them stick. Would serve Evershaw right. But Carter didn't retreat, instead moving until he could lean his fists on the desk. "Listen to me, Evershaw, and hear me well. We know you're working up some scheme against Blood-Moon pack, and we're watching."

Evershaw's head tilted slowly and a predator looked out from his eyes. "You challenging me, Chase?"

"You face Rafe and Ruby fairly. No tricks, no bullshit. And let a fair contest decide the results, if you can't trust the Council. Stop fucking scheming like a teenaged girl."

The wolf's lip curled. "What the fuck do you know about fair? Life isn't fair, little kitty. Get used to it."

Carter's lion roared and rattled his brain, and enough of it echoed in his chest that Evershaw looked the smallest bit less confident. Not concerned, not worried, just less confident. Carter reined in the rage and gripped the edge of the desk until the wood creaked. "Fight fair, Evershaw. Be a man. She's worked too damn hard for what she's got to lose it because of a fucking cheater."

"You ready to fight for Ruby?" When Carter hesitated, Evershaw seized the advantage and lurched forward, knocking Carter back. "You think I don't know? You think I didn't see it? Give me a break. You're fucking her. What, think you're going to get your own little wolf pack? Stand up on your own, since Logan won't let you play leader? I'll negotiate with you, too, Chase. If you speak for Ruby, fuck it. We can settle this right now."

"I don't speak for Ruby." Carter snarled and his nails darkened, the lion on the verge of bursting forth whether he intended to shift or not. Not even Eloise's muttered warning caught his attention as he lifted the desk and heaved it aside. That son of a bitch. That lowly son of a bitch. "Don't you dare threaten her. Don't you fucking *dare*, I'll kill you in your own den, I'll —"

"What the fuck is going on in here?" Ruby's voice rang out, cutting through his words with devastating precision.

The only person in the entire city who could cut through the fog of fury in his brain stormed in, and Carter faced her, panicked that she walked into SilverLine's den without protection, but thrilled she would end this thing with Evershaw. He growled, about to reach for her so they could present a united front against the SilverLine alpha, but froze as Ruby turned on him.

She wasn't pissed at Evershaw. Not at all. Her fist connected with Carter's chest instead, and her eyes flashed gold as she rounded on him. "What the fuck are you doing here? What do you think you're doing?"

"Evershaw tried to call in —"

"Are you messing in pack business?" Her features changed, grew more wolf-like, and dark fur sprouted on the backs of her arms as she whaled another punch into his side. "I *told* you. I told you this was the one thing I couldn't —"

She turned away, refusing to look at him. "Get the fuck out of here. I'm done."

Carter couldn't breathe. He couldn't do anything but look at her. He could explain. He could fix it. But she wouldn't look at him.

And Evershaw's smug expression only made him feel worse. Angrier. More helpless.

Carter stepped forward, reaching for Ruby's arm, but Eloise caught his attention and shook her head. The Medusa dragged him out of the building, saying under her breath, "Don't get involved in the wolf business, man," and nothing else, until they were outside and in the car.

Carter stared at the steering wheel, numb from his hair to the tips of his fingers. Ruby thought he'd interfered in pack business. It was over. His lion stalked and paced, ready to fight for her. He wouldn't just let her disappear. She had to listen to him. Had to.

Eloise didn't move or tell him to start the car. Her hair settled down, and one long braid tickled his shoulder, as if to comfort him. "So you and Ruby were seeing each other?"

"Sort of." His voice came out rusty and broken. He took a deep breath and started the car. "But not anymore."

"I bet Natalia could…"

He just shook his head. He might be able to fix it, but getting Natalia involved would only complicate things further. Neither of them spoke for the drive back to the office, or the elevator ride up to Benedict's office. He might not want to reveal his relationship with Ruby, but his brothers deserved to know what Evershaw planned. At least then the Council would not be caught unawares by the coyotes. It didn't make him feel any better.

chapter 15

I saw red the moment I walked into Evershaw's office and found Carter there, snarling about fighting and settling things with Evershaw. That lion jackass thought he could fight my battles for me. Went to my enemy to try to head things off and protect me – without asking permission, or my opinion, or anything. He just did it. Typical.

By the time Eloise dragged Carter out of the office and Todd quietly excused himself, I still couldn't see straight. Evershaw stood next to his desk chair, though the desk stood on its end across the room. No doubt from Carter's temper. I bared my teeth. "What the fuck are you doing, Evershaw?"

"Eloise owed me a favor. I called it in. I didn't ask Chase to come here, he just showed up with her. I have no business with him." Evershaw looked older suddenly, but that didn't make him any less dangerous. "But I have business with you."

"Look," I said, wanting to throw something at him just to see some kind of emotion on his face. The man was as expressive as a chalkboard. "I know you're trying to get the jackals and hyenas with you to try to get rid of my pack. I see it, Miles. You're not that sneaky, and it's a small city."

"I wasn't trying to be sneaky." He crossed his arms and watched me. "That wasn't the point. The point was to demonstrate to you the lengths to which I will go to secure power in this city – for myself and for you. Yes, I want my pack to be the lead pack in this city. And I want you to be the alpha female of that pack. What happens to Blood-Moon and Rafe, I don't care. If the Council votes the way I suspect they will, there will be a single wolf pack in this city. Rafe can move outside the city limits and try suburban life, or he can swear fealty to us. Either way, we would be in charge. That's how it should be, Ruby."

I shook my head, even though Carter's betrayal made Evershaw's offer more tempting. I would never write off Natalia, but the Chase brothers could go fuck themselves. Only the wolves, working as a single unit, could hope to offset the power of the lion pride. "We won't just give up, Evershaw. We'll fight you, alpha to alpha, to decide rank among the packs. It shouldn't be up to the Council. This is between wolves, it should stay among wolves. Why the fuck would you ask the lions and bears and hyenas to vote on who we should be?"

"Because you wouldn't see reason." Irritation narrowed his eyes. "I gave you plenty of time, Ruby. But since you'd rather fuck around with the lions, I had to take another route."

The blood drained from my face so quickly I swayed, almost embarrassed myself and lost my rank by fainting. Sheer stubbornness kept me upright in the face of Evershaw's grim triumph. "Did he tell you that?"

"Of course he didn't." Evershaw righted his desk in jerky movements, still riled up, and started collecting all the shit that had flown off. "It's obvious. It was obvious a week ago in the gym."

My heart sank. If it was obvious to everyone else, then it couldn't only be an infatuation. Maybe it meant more, and I would never be able to escape the draw of Carter Chase. I couldn't move, watching him stoop to gather up the pieces of his computer. "You don't know what you're talking about."

Evershaw shot me a dark look. "Grow up, Ruby. Whatever it is, it won't last. He's a lion. You're a wolf. You should be with a wolf. He will never understand you. He will never understand how a pack works, or what it means to be a pack. The lions pretend like they know, but they're too different."

He said exactly what my own doubtful head told me, despite that my heart remained steadfast. Even knowing why Evershaw would say those things to me, I almost believed him. Feared he was right, regardless of what my heart said. "I'm not interested in…"

"The Council will decide where we go from here. Unless you want to accept my offer?" Evershaw shook his head as he studied his computer monitor and placed it on the desk. "If we team up, Ruby, everything changes."

"You won't blackmail me into mating with you." I clenched my fists at my sides.

"It's not blackmail. It's not a threat." He sighed and collapsed back into his chair, looking too tired to be threatening. "You're an adult. Make your own damn choice. I'm doing what I have to in order to keep my pack strong and on top. I'd expect no less from you."

"Fine." I channeled the fury and hurt of Carter's betrayal and gritted my teeth. "Ditch the underhanded shit, Evershaw. I'll face you, alpha to alpha, and we'll decide this by the old laws. Fight to first blood."

He opened his mouth to argue, or say he wouldn't fight me, or proposition me again, but I stormed out before he could speak. I'd had enough of Miles Evershaw. And I'd had enough of Carter Chase. Men in general, really. I stormed through the warehouse, ignoring Todd as he tried to get my attention, and flung open the steel door to the outside until it banged off the wall and almost shut in my face.

Outside, I called Natalia and asked her to meet me at the bar. She might know more about this. Whatever the Chases planned, if Nat knew and didn't tell me, then I had a pretty clear idea of who I could rely on in the coming week. The Council would vote to establish a single pack or to let the wolves sort it out among themselves, and we would have to live by their decision.

I rode the motorcycle more recklessly than normal, white lining and cutting off cars on the crowded city streets, but I didn't care. Carter betrayed me. Went to Evershaw to talk about pack business. Which only cemented how Evershaw saw me – a prize to be won or stolen, some trophy he could take from the lions to decorate his pack. I gritted my teeth as I strode into the bar, heading for the office so I could confront my brother.

Rafe stared at a spreadsheet so hard I thought I smelled something burning, but he looked up as I stormed in. "What the hell, Bee?"

"We have a problem."

"Does that problem have anything to do with Edgar Chase sitting upstairs, waiting for you?"

My heart seized up. But he said Edgar, not Carter. And I could face Edgar any day of the week. The security chief pretended to be tough as nails, but in reality there was a genuinely nice guy inside. I raked a hand through my hair as I stared around the office, not quite ready to go face Edgar. "It might. Evershaw called in his favor from Eloise. I don't know what he asked for, but it will be bad for us."

"Then we should challenge Evershaw now, before the Council gives a verdict. At least we have some control over the situation," I said.

"If we challenge him, we're the instigators. Makes him look like the victim," Rafe returned.

Rafe snorted, leaning back in the chair. He watched me for a long time before he went on. "What were you doing at Evershaw's, anyway? Are you two involved?"

"Don't be ridiculous." My stomach flipped at the thought. "I went there to confront Evershaw about all the shit he's doing, stirring up the jackals and coyotes and hyenas against us."

"You went to SilverLine territory, into his *den*, without telling me? Without asking me to go with you?" Rafe sat forward, expression difficult to decipher.

I took a deep breath. "Yes, but —"

"Fuck, Ruby." He lurched to his feet to pace. "We work together. That's how this works. If you start going off to negotiate with other packs without me, you're undermining my authority. Just because you're a better fighter doesn't mean you're the top dog. We both bring strengths to this pack. That's why this works. But it obviously doesn't work if you feel like you can take on an entire pack by yourself, and you don't even bother telling me you're going to do it."

"Rafe," I said, then cut off. He was right, after all. I scrubbed my hands over my face. Everything was falling apart. Everything. "I'm sorry. I got too focused on being pissed at Evershaw. I didn't think."

"No, you didn't." He turned his attention back to the computer. "Go talk to Edgar. I need to take a minute before I say something I regret."

The wolf snarled in the back of my head, but I couldn't tell if she was angrier with me or him. So I turned on my heel and walked away without another word, slamming my fist into the door as I passed. My heart ached as I climbed the stairs to the living room, dreading seeing Edgar. I just wanted to curl up in my bed and hold the pillow that still smelled like Carter. It had been too perfect.

Edgar sat in the recliner that faced the stairs, so he saw me when I finally dragged myself around the corner. His eyebrow arched when he caught sight of me. "You okay, Ruby?"

"No." I leaned back against the wall but didn't want to get any closer. He looked just enough like Carter that I might lose my good sense and admit something I shouldn't. "But I don't want to talk about it. What do you want, Edgar?"

The other eyebrow joined the first. "Logan sent me. SilverLine called another emergency session of the Council for tonight. Something about the coyotes joining. John and his crew are ready to accept Council membership. Logan wanted to make sure you and Rafe knew and were able to attend."

My lungs seized and I couldn't breathe. The coyotes unbalanced the Council relationships. They'd support Evershaw, without a doubt. I rubbed my forehead and wondered for the first time if I could just walk away. Leave the pack, leave Rafe, leave Carter, leave everything behind. Find a new city without all this bullshit drama and start over. Being alpha had been fun. And it had been my goal for so long that I had no idea what to do after achieving it. Managing a pack was headache after headache.

When the silence stretched and I couldn't speak, Edgar rose and shoved his hands in his pockets. He got that thoughtful expression that usually meant trouble, and the lion paced toward me with more scrutiny than my wolf liked. "Did something happen today, Ruby? You don't look surprised that the coyotes are joining."

"I had a conversation with Evershaw today. He was planning something. I figured it would be something like this."

Edgar didn't buy it. But at least he didn't call me on the half-truth. He glanced at his watch, then headed for the stairs. "Let me know if you need to talk about anything, Ruby. We'll see you at the Council meeting tonight at eight."

I didn't say anything as he left. Instead, I collapsed onto the leather couch and buried my face in one of the blankets. Running away seemed like the best idea I'd had all week.

chapter 16

Logan listened without comment as Carter tried to explain the last couple of weeks – his relationship with Ruby, the conflict with Evershaw, and the earlier confrontation over Eloise's favor. The gorgon hovered near the door of Logan's office, her hair out of control as she hugged herself and paced. Carter tried to keep emotion out of his voice, but his heart broke, and his lion mourned. His mate felt betrayed. By *him*.

Logan leaned his elbows on his desk and covered his face, sighing so heavily Carter thought he might deflate. The alpha spoke to no one in particular. "I just sent Edgar to O'Shea's to tell Rafe and Ruby about the emergency Council session tonight. The coyotes agreed to join the Council, and will take the oath."

Carter shook his head, lurching forward. "They can't. Evershaw is using them to get a majority…"

“We’ve demanded all shifters in the city cooperate with the Council, or pay the price. We can’t turn the coyotes away when they’ve finally agreed to do what we told them to do.” Logan massaged his temples.

Eloise cleared her throat. “I’m sorry, Logan. I promised him a favor but I didn’t think —”

“It’s not your fault.” Logan leaned back in his chair and stared up at the ceiling. “Go check in with Benedict, El. So he doesn’t kill Carter for taking you to see Todd Evershaw.”

She made a face and reached for the door. “Jesus Christ, will I never live that down?” She slammed the door behind her without another word or a backward glance, and something in Carter’s chest eased. He could be more honest with just Logan in the room.

His eldest brother fixed him with a no bullshit look. “The whole story, Car. Not the after school special version.”

“She’s my mate.” The words escaped in a rush and a weight lifted off his shoulders. Finally, finally, he could say it aloud in front of others. He lurched to his feet and started pacing. “Ruby is my mate. She’s…worried about what it would look like, if we were together, so I agreed to a trial run. Evershaw wants her as a business deal, a way to consolidate power without giving a shit how she feels. I went with Eloise to protect her, but also to…look out for Ruby.”

“Evershaw wouldn’t look past the opportunity to make the choice easier for her. As long as it was the choice to go with him.” Logan stifled a groan.

“Yeah.” Carter shook his head, wishing he had something to hit. “And when she came in, she heard enough that she thought…she had to think I betrayed her trust and went to Evershaw on her behalf. I didn't, Logan. I wouldn't."

"I know, Carter."

"What do I do?" Carter faced his brother in desperation, hands clenched at his sides. "Logan, how do I fix this? She's my mate. I can't lose her."

Logan's stoic expression softened a touch, and he took a deep breath. "Well, I sure as shit don't know how to calm a furious woman down. Why do you think I'm here so much? Half the time I say the wrong thing and hide out here until Nat forgets about it, or the flowers and chocolate distract her."

Carter frowned at him, wanting real advice, but Logan held up his hands. "So keep that in mind. Give her a little time to cool off. Talk to Natalia about what to say. Maybe call Rafe. And then you have to talk to Ruby, brother. You can't force her to accept you. A woman like that, an alpha… she'll just dig in her heels if you try to convince her. But you have to fight for your mate."

Carter stared at him, a thousand possibilities running through his mind, and tried to imagine a future where Ruby wasn't part of his life. "Can I get her back?"

Logan picked up his cell phone and fussed with it, finally holding it up to his ear though he spoke to Carter. "Let's find out."

It rang for a long time before Natalia picked up, and from the look on Logan's face, she wasn't happy. The alpha even held the phone away from his ear so Carter could hear Natalia ranting about jackass lions, and insensitive pricks, and belligerent males always interfering in her business. Logan listened for some time, making agreeing noises whenever Nat paused to take a breath, and eventually she trailed off to only spitting curses.

Logan sounded mild and barely interested. "Babe, please listen to me."

From the way the alpha flinched, the response was not positive. Carter held his breath. Logan rubbed his forehead and rolled his eyes, still trying to sound soothing. "I know, babe. I know. We can talk more about that later, okay? Now, though, I need you to listen to me. What happened wasn't what Ruby thinks happened."

And again Logan held the phone away from his ear as Natalia's voice gained both decibels and octaves. Carter leaned back against the wall and stared out the enormous windows behind Logan's desk at the city below. Maybe it was over. He would have to leave the city. Maybe the country. And that wouldn't be enough distance to forget the scent of Ruby's perfume, the feel of her skin. He would have to die inside, just to keep breathing.

Logan watched him, then said to the phone, despite that Nat continued shouting at him, "Ask Eloise. Eloise was there. If you don't believe me, your *mate*, call the damn gorgon. I love you, even though you're being completely unreasonable, and I will see you at home tonight." Then he hung up and shoved to his feet, striding over to Carter. "Brother, don't look like that. Please don't look like that."

And then his arms crushed around Carter and Carter couldn't breathe. Couldn't think. He stared over Logan's shoulder as the alpha tried to squeeze the grief right out of him, and managed to say, "What if I lose her?"

"You won't." Logan pounded his back. "You won't. Come on, man."

Carter didn't believe him.

chapter 17

Two hours of crying and shouting and arguing left me with a bitch of a headache. Natalia tried to make me feel better, but after Logan called, she was more distracted by what a dick *he* was than helping me see whether Carter was just as bad. I felt like an ice pick was stabbed through my temple as Rafe and I left for the Council meeting. Nat still fumed at the bar, unwilling to go back to the mansion to deal with Logan or Carter or any of the lions, though she grudgingly admitted she'd promised Eloise truffles, and would have to go back to make them.

In the car on the way to the meeting, Rafe stared out the windshield and gripped the steering wheel until his knuckles whitened. He didn't say anything and I wallowed in my own misery, watching the city slide by. Rafe parked the car but didn't cut the engine or get out. He sat there for so long I almost expected him to kick me out.

Finally, he exhaled in a gust but wouldn't look at me. "Carter called me."

I was too tired to be angry. "I'm not surprised."

"He said to talk to Eloise. Evershaw set them both up, and us." Rafe finally looked at me, his expression lost in the dark shadows. "What's the plan, Bee?"

Hearing the familiar nickname just made me feel worse. I'd betrayed his trust. I took a deep breath, shifting in the seat until I could face him full on. "I'm sorry, Rafe. For everything. I got so caught up in finding Carter that I lost sight of what's best for the pack, and..."

"I don't really give a shit about the pack, Ruby." I blinked and my brother held up a hand to cut me off. "We can hand the pack over to Evershaw tonight and be across state lines before anyone knows. You're my sister, and I love you. I want what's best for you. Tell me what's best for Ruby, and that's what we do. Stop thinking about the pack."

My eyes stung but I felt all cried out. I managed to squeeze his hand. "I don't know what's best for me. I don't know anymore."

He sighed. "Okay. Then our goal for tonight is to delay. Regardless of what Evershaw, or the lions, or the rest of the Council says, we stall. A vote, a fight, whatever. We stall. Next week. That gives us more time to plan, and for you to think."

"Rafe, I'm really sorry. I don't know how things got so screwed up."

My brother attempted a smile. "It's probably my fault, too. I should have kicked Carter's ass the second I caught him staring at yours, six years ago."

I blinked. "You what?"

"Jesus, Ruby, he's loved you for years. He's quiet about it, though. I didn't say anything because I didn't think he had the balls to ask you out. Good for him." Rafe shut off the car and kicked his door open. "Let's get this over with."

I checked myself in the mirror to make sure I didn't look like death warmed over, though my eyes were still puffy, and followed Rafe into the Council's meeting rooms. We couldn't face Evershaw or the other alphas with anything less than our strongest defense.

Inside, the halls were quiet and dim, barely lit. Each alpha had an office in the hall, but we bypassed our pack's office in favor of the meeting chambers at the far end of the hall. Most of the alphas already gathered, and the coyotes sat in the center of the circle of tables. They looked just a tiny bit nervous.

I refused to look at Logan, Edgar, or Benedict where they sat next to us, though Rafe went to shake Logan's hand, and instead seated myself to stare straight ahead. I didn't have anything to say to anyone. We had business to conduct, and the sooner we made it clear where Blood-Moon stood, the sooner we could get the hell out of there and start preparing to take Miles Evershaw down.

The SilverLine alpha sat across the circle from us, unfortunately in my line of sight, with Todd next to him. Evershaw's famously impassive visage only made me hate him more. The man might as well have been cut from stone for all the emotion he displayed. I could have respected him more if he at least looked gleeful about the trouble he would cause. But no. He sat with his arms across his chest and watched the coyote alpha, John, with as much interest as a man watching grass grow.

Rafe eased into the chair next to mine but said nothing. No reason to show our cards so early in the meeting. I pushed away every shred of emotion and did my best Evershaw impression as the other alphas filed in and took their seats. The hyena queen, one of Eloise's friends, looked about as happy to be in the room as I felt.

Kaiser spoke first, big and gruff and calm, as he lumbered to his feet and leaned forward. The table creaked under his weight, and I wondered whether any of the furniture had been reinforced to account for shifter strength. Probably not, by the way it wobbled. Kaiser scanned the room, his eyes narrowed, to take in every alpha there. "The coyotes wish to join the Council as members, and have sworn to adhere to the guidelines and rulings of the Council." His gaze paused on Rafe and I before he went on. "That is the matter before us, and that is the only matter we will be discussing tonight. Everything else can wait until the next scheduled Council meeting, three weeks from now."

Maybe Logan bought us some time. Or maybe Kaiser remembered what he'd told me, what felt like another lifetime ago in his gym — Evershaw was dangerous for me, too. I refused to react, though.

John, the skinny coyote leader, addressed the assembled alphas with a winning smile. "The coyote collective is pleased to join the Council. We agree to abide by the judgments of the Council, and will adhere to the standards of conduct as outlined by the Council."

Logan's voice rumbled into the quiet room, and he managed to sound irritated as well as disinterested. "So you will cease organizing and profiting from illegal street-fights?"

The coyote's smile broadened, but he held his hands out in an almost helpless gesture. "We could, but it turns out we supply an entertainment option that is in high demand. We wouldn't want to cut off the fighters who profit from our enterprise, or the spectators who so enjoy each sporting event."

"Pitting unwitting humans against shifters is not sporting." Kaiser's fingers drummed a sharp tattoo on the table. "Much like a coyote baiting a bear is not sporting. Don't you agree?"

John didn't even blink, his conman skills bubbling up as he took an offended air and a wounded tone. "I would never bait the bears, Kaiser, and I'm disappointed you feel that way. And we go to great lengths to make sure the humans aren't in any real danger. We even employ a gorgon as insurance against anyone going berserk. Well, we used to employ a gorgon, until the Chases stole her away," and he shook a finger at Benedict, as if the lawyer was a naughty kid and not a lion about ready to shift to protect his mate.

A snarl broke the silence as Benedict leaned forward over the table. "Stole? *Stole*?"

"A coyote baiting a lion is also pretty stupid," Kaiser said, as Edgar gripped his brother's shoulder to keep Benedict from launching at the grinning coyote alpha. The bear did not look impressed. "And since Eloise is no longer in your employ, how do you propose to run fights that are illegal but will not get any humans killed?"

"We're re-evaluating our business model and security posture." John's grin never slipped. "And look forward to the Council's input on our way forward."

Lacey, the hyena queen, folded her arms over her chest. "And if the Council voted you must cease organizing and supporting these fights?"

"The collective would respectfully petition the Council to develop alternate revenue streams." John faced her until I could no longer see his expression, though I wanted to throw something at the back of his head. "Unfortunately, the fights sustain the entire collective. If those earnings went away, we would be in dire straits. Most dire."

"The Council will not provide welfare because your illegal business is put out of operation." This from the jackal alpha, a grizzled older man with his son Harrison by his side. Sam Armstrong didn't take shit from anyone, and his attitude only grew colder and angrier after the death of his youngest son, Cal. It was still so recent that the jackals occasionally retreated from the Council as they debated how to heal their pack internally. Sam gripped the edge of the table as he watched the coyote alpha hem and haw.

John finally inclined his head at the jackal. "Point well taken, Armstrong. We're developing other investments to take the place of the fights."

Rafe glanced at me, about to speak, but Logan beat him to it. The lion alpha started gathering his papers, preparing to leave. "Fine. When you're ready to stop conducting illegal fights, we will be ready to readdress your petition to join the Council. We're not going to accept a criminal enterprise into the governing council."

"Funny, coming from the biggest criminal in the room," Evershaw said, and I blinked. Rafe tensed beside me, and leaned away from where the lions sat on his left.

Logan's teeth glinted in the light, and a gold shadow crossed his eyes. "Tread lightly, Evershaw."

The wolf shrugged. "Your business skirts the law, Chase. Bends it, interprets it, breaks it. You steal from the poor, and gather more wealth for yourself and your friends. You do nothing to contribute to society. At least John is providing housing, food, healthcare, and other necessities for his people and strays in the city."

A chorus of growls rose from the lion table, and I allowed a bit of hope to grow in my chest. Evershaw only alienated the rest of the Council by antagonizing the Chase brothers and supporting the fights. Sure, some shifters made money fighting in abandoned warehouses, including Atticus Chase and his mate Sophia, but every fight increased the risk of the humans discovering shifters existed.

Logan bristled, the shoulders of his suit straining as he flexed. "You know nothing about my business, Evershaw, and if you defame me again, we can handle this in the traditional manner."

Which meant fighting to the death in animal form. I almost hoped it would come to that. I had no doubt who would win that fight. But Evershaw wouldn't antagonize the lions without a backup plan.

Evershaw didn't look particularly concerned. "Truth isn't defamation. That aside, I will vouch for the coyotes. They will cease the illegal fights within sixty days, or you may hold me accountable for their failure and any penalties levied against them. Will that assuage the Council's concerns?"

Kaiser looked between the lion and the wolf, then heaved a sigh. "Not entirely, but it's a start. We'll put it to the vote, then. The bears do not oppose allowing the coyotes provisional status with the Council, to be reviewed in thirty days."

My stomach clenched and I dug my nails into my thigh to keep from turning and snapping curses at the bear leader. Son of a bitch. How could he vote in support of those bastards?

Logan didn't blink. "The Pride is opposed. Strongly."

And then it was our turn. Rafe folded his arms over his chest. "BloodMoon opposes. Equally strongly."

John, still standing in the middle of the Council, just grinned at me, unconcerned. Like the outcome was already set. I hated the feeling of inevitability that swept through me. As if I watched a movie, and could identify the exact turning point when everything started falling apart.

Lacey, the hyena queen, stared at the coyote leader for a very long time before she voted. "We will support the new membership, contingent on all illegal fights ending within sixty days."

It grew more difficult to breathe, my heart in my throat.

Sam Armstrong shook his head. "Fine. Sixty days to prove yourself, coyote." He pronounced it "kah-yote," the last syllable clipped with ill-concealed anger.

And with that, and Evershaw's supportive vote, we lost.

John executed a partial bow to the Council, shook Evershaw's hand, then eyed the assembled alphas. "We'd like to raise a motion to create a single representative for each species. There's another group of coyotes operating outside the city, and if they were to try and join the Council, it would create tension and strife."

Kaiser's expression soured. "Don't push your luck, coyote. As I said, your status is the only issue we will address tonight, and…"

"SilverLine seconds the motion to create a single representative to vote on behalf of the rest of their kind. Chase votes for the felines already. It doesn't make sense to have multiple wolf packs and coyote groups. Any fool can create a pack and claim they need status with the Council. The next thing you know, we'll be as unwieldy and ineffective as the federal government." Evershaw eased to his feet, making eye contact with each alpha as he spoke. "What if more bears showed up in the city but wanted to remain loners? Should each lone bear have a voting position with the Council? No. We need to limit the voting members, and the best way to limit it is by species. One vote per species."

The bear grumbled as he scowled at Evershaw. "We're not getting into this now, Evershaw. If there's trouble between the wolves, we will deal with it at the next meeting."

"Very well." The wolf alpha didn't look disappointed. "So long as it is on the agenda, we can table the discussion until then. But we will certainly address it."

So we had three weeks to figure out how to stonewall Evershaw. How to convince the rest of the Council this was just an insane grab for power. Before Kaiser could even close the meeting, I shoved my chair back and walked out. Three weeks wasn't enough time. If we weren't strong enough to meet and overturn Evershaw's challenge in three weeks, it would be the end of BloodMoon pack.

chapter 18

Carter tried yoga. He tried meditating. He tried beating the shit out of a punching bag in the gym at the mansion. When none of that kept his mind off Ruby and the Council meeting, he retreated to the kitchen for beer and something deep-fried or covered in chocolate.

He found Eloise and Natalia deep in conversation, which stopped the moment he appeared. Carter nodded to Nat as he headed to the fridge, "I'm just getting a beer, I'll get out of your hair in..."

"Sit down." The chef's voice didn't give him much confidence it would be a pleasant conversation for him, so Carter put the beer back and got a bottle of whiskey from the cupboard instead.

Eloise snorted, swinging her feet against the cupboard where she sat on the counter, and tossed a towel at him. "Want a blindfold before you face the executioner?"

He gave her a sideways look and used the towel to mop up a puddle on the island as he pulled out a stool. He poured himself more whiskey than he normally would, and put about half of it down before he could face Natalia.

She wore an apron dotted with chocolate and spattered with flour and other baking ingredients, and a bit of flour dusted her cheek as well. But she looked ready for battle as she waved a whisk at him. "Eloise has been trying to explain what the fuck went on today, and I've already heard from Ruby what *she* saw and heard. Logan said you wanted to fix this. If that's true, then start talking."

Carter finished the rest of his drink and poured another. Sometimes liquor worked better than yoga and meditation, combined. It was only a temporary fix, but at least if he was drunk he could get a little sleep. The weight of their attention made him shift his own weight on the stool. It would be easier just to talk to Benedict and Logan, and even Atticus. But Natalia was the only one with a direct line to Ruby. He studied his hands on the smooth quartz countertop. "Eloise asked me to go with her to talk to Evershaw. I went. I lost my temper with Evershaw and told him to fight fair if he planned something against Ruby."

"Did you get involved in pack business?"

Carter wanted to deny it immediately, but he took his time to weigh what he'd said and done. "That wasn't my intention. I wanted to keep Evershaw from being an underhanded shitbag. That was it."

Natalia narrowed her eyes as she watched him, stirring a double boiler on the stove. "Did you tell Evershaw to stay away from Ruby?"

"I wanted to." His hand closed around the bottle of whiskey. He envisioned chucking it across the kitchen, watching the bottle explode against the cabinets. But he just dumped more into his glass and got up to put the bottle away. "But I didn't."

Natalia took the chocolate off the stove and began to drizzle it over little truffle things on a baking sheet on the counter. She only paused to smack Eloise when the gorgon stole a truffle and scooted across the kitchen. Natalia went back to the dessert, her back to him so Carter couldn't read her expression as she spoke. "Just you being there, talking about Ruby at all, is interfering in pack business. That's the problem, Carter. If you don't see it, you…"

"I told him to fight fair." Carter gripped the edge of the counter and tried to keep his tone even. Shouting at Natalia would mean a very quick death if Logan ever found out. "And there is no one on this planet who could convince me to let some asshole like Miles Evershaw take advantage of my mate. Even you. Even *her*."

He ground his teeth so loudly he didn't even notice the silence. When he looked up, Natalia stared at him, chocolate forgotten as her spoon dripped all over the floor, and Eloise plundered the truffles with impunity. Nat shook her head. "Your what?"

"My mate." Carter laughed, but it had an ugly edge to it that he hated. "Oh, Ruby didn't tell you that part? She's my mate. I'm pretty sure I'm hers, but she won't admit it. Ruby O'Shea is my mate. I wanted to pick Miles Evershaw up by the throat and crush him for the things he's said to her, the way he's treated her, but I didn't. I *didn't*. It took every ounce of control I possess – and a hell of a lot of meditation – but I managed not to kill him in his own den. And now she won't even speak to me."

Natalia spluttered, looking at Eloise before returning her attention to Carter. "Your mate?"

"Yeah." Carter leaned his elbows on the counter, fixing her with a hard stare as his lion rumbled, and his voice dropped. "So think about what it would take for Logan to stand aside quietly as some douchebag like Miles Evershaw propositioned you like you were a business deal, and then started doing underhanded shit to try to drag you down? What would he do?"

Natalia's lips compressed to a thin line and she looked away.

"Right," Carter said. "I helped clean up the mess at the soup kitchen, so I guess we both know what he would do. And yet Miles Evershaw lives. He lives. I deserve some fucking credit for that."

"You've got it," Edgar said from the doorway, looking grim as he walked into the kitchen and retrieved a beer from the fridge. "And I also deserve some credit for not killing Evershaw. Logan really does, too. Benedict, not so much."

The lawyer loosened his tie as he strode over to Eloise. "Shut up, Edgar."

Logan already pinched the bridge of his nose as he followed behind Benedict, but he went to Natalia to kiss her forehead and check her over before he turned blue-gold eyes on Carter. "The coyotes are in a probationary membership to the Council now. And BloodMoon has three weeks until the Council addresses who will represent each group."

Carter stared at his whiskey, wishing he still had the bottle. "Evershaw behaved himself?"

Edgar snorted as he pulled out the stool next to Carter and slapped his back. "Of course he didn't. Called Logan a criminal."

Natalia untangled herself from Logan's embrace and started cleaning up the chocolate on the floor. She sounded flustered as she scrubbed. "How was Ruby? Did she say anything?"

"No." Logan frowned as he pulled her upright to hold against his side. "And leave that, the maids can clean it up later. Ruby didn't do anything but sit there."

Carter wanted to flee, with three of his brothers watching him closely. The silence stretched as they waited, and Natalia finally blurted out, "Ruby is his mate. They're mates. What happens if she doesn't forgive him?"

"Depends," Edgar said, when no one else spoke. Eloise looked at the floor, and Benedict edged closer to her with a worried grumble. Logan's arm tightened around Nat and he got a faraway look. Edgar spoke as if he gave her the weather forecast. "She's still around. He could torture himself by staying here and seeing her every day, but not being able to have her. He could leave and torture himself knowing she's here, alone and unprotected. They will both spend the rest of their lives knowing there is a hole in their heart, something missing from their soul. That life could have been a thousand times better, more real, more colorful. It would be the difference between living in black and white, and living in color. It's like not being able to feel any warmth unless you stick your hand in a fire, not being able to taste anything, or smell anything."

Edgar's voice never changed but Carter couldn't swallow, staring down at the counter and praying he didn't bolt for the car to drive to O'Shea's to convince Ruby she was wrong. He had to get her back. He couldn't live like that.

"How do you know that, Edgar?" Natalia's voice cracked, as if she already knew the answer to her question. Logan held her tighter still, pressing his face to her hair.

Carter watched Edgar in his peripheral vision, holding his breath. Edgar never talked about it. Never talked about her. They knew better than to bring it up. It was too terrible, too impossible to comprehend, or understand, or even just hear.

But Edgar's expression didn't harden. He didn't break or grow angry. He sounded resigned, tired. Even the smile that tugged at the corner of his mouth looked just a little sad. "Because my mate died in a car accident twelve years ago."

Nat's eyes brimmed with tears and then overflowed, and even caustic Eloise dashed at her cheeks.

Edgar knocked his knuckles on the counter and eased to his feet. "So I know whereof I speak, Natalia. It's a shitty way to live, and I wouldn't wish it on either Ruby or Carter."

"You can't do this to a pregnant woman," Natalia said, too loudly, and lurched forward to hug him tightly. She cried on his shoulder while Edgar stood and patted her back, but Edgar had long since stopped crying over his lost mate. Carter remembered the exact day Ed stopped crying, because that was the day Ed stopped feeling almost everything.

Nat hiccupped and punched Edgar's side, pushing him away to sniffle and wipe at her nose. "You never said anything. And you let us walk around here in love, and hugging, and happy, and you just…you didn't say anything. How can you stand it? How can you stand seeing us together?"

Carter couldn't breathe, let his head fall forward on his arms so he might not hear Edgar's response. Carter didn't want to face a future like Edgar's, always alone. Always wondering what if. Always angry at the universe and fate or whatever took his mate away. And Carter would still have to face Ruby, knowing their life together would be amazing but still unable to have it. He didn't know what would be worse.

Edgar patted her back and directed her to Logan, agitated by Nat's tears. Logan immediately engulfed her in an embrace. Edgar retrieved the bottle of whiskey from the cupboard and poured a bit more for Carter before he took a deep swig, right from the bottle. He capped it and held it up for Nat to see. "I drink. A lot."

"Does it help?" Carter asked, not lifting his head.

"Not really." Edgar squeezed his shoulder. "So we'll get you sorted, Carter."

"Yes." Natalia's voice barely escaped from Logan's arms.

No one said anything, no one made eye contact, for a long moment. Benedict finally straightened from his lean against the counter, and looked at Natalia. "Did you just say you're pregnant?"

Logan sighed. "Yes."

Benedict looked around the room, expression comical. "Did everyone know but me? What the hell, Logan?"

"You explain," Edgar said to Logan, then reached out to drag Carter to his feet. "Little brother and I will take a walk."

Carter went with him, struggling to breathe. Edgar would know how to fix it. Edgar would find a way, he always did.

chapter 19

I met Nat a few days later at the designer's shop for her final dress fitting. I felt like nine miles of bad road, with a constant migraine and a short temper. Rafe and I spent every waking moment at the bar or the office, searching for ways to challenge Evershaw's assertion. We reached out to the jackals, the hyenas, the bears, a few stray wolves roaming the city, and every other shifter we could find to try and gauge their interest in supporting us over Evershaw. He had a good argument, though, and none of the other alphas wanted to see their power diluted.

So I wasn't in the mood to gossip and giggle as I dragged myself into the designer's fitting rooms. Not that Nat wanted to giggle. She looked pale and wan, almost uneasy as I walked in, and she wobbled to her feet to hug me. "How are you?"

"I've been better." I attempted a smile and flopped onto the chaise. "There's a lot of work to be done."

She waited until the designer retreated to face me from the dais, wearing her beautiful gown. "Have you talked to Evershaw? Or Carter?"

"No and no." I covered my eyes, feeling tired to my bones. With each passing hour, walking away seemed better and better. The stress would kill me before Evershaw got a chance. "Rafe and I have been busy trying to make friends."

"Logan said it isn't clear which way the Council will go."

"Oh, it's plenty clear." I rubbed my forehead and couldn't meet her gaze. "They'll side with Evershaw. He's giving them a case for maintaining their power later. If more bears or lions or jackals move in, Evershaw's stance gives Kaiser, and Logan, and Armstrong the precedent to force those newcomers to swear fealty. They'd have to be stupid to side with us."

Natalia swallowed hard, dry-washing her hands in front of her, and her eyes grew red. "What are you going to do?"

Resignation crept over me. I'd fought it for the last few days, and the two weeks before that, but it felt inevitable. Evershaw would win. Rafe and I would have to deal with the fall-out. We just didn't know what that looked like. "I don't know. Sell the bar and leave?"

She stumbled off the dais and nearly tripped on her skirt as she tried to hug me. "You can't."

"We'll stick around until the Council meeting, so I can still be your maid of honor." I tried to smile. "So don't worry about that."

"I wasn't, you idiot." Natalia gingerly sat on the chaise next to me, fussing with the gown and the skirt and the neckline, and shook her head. "You can beat Evershaw in a fight, though. If it comes down to it, can't you just demand trial by combat and finish things up that way?"

"Maybe." I shoved to my feet so I could undress and get into my gown. I tried not to remember the last time I'd tried it on, when the evidence of Carter's passion covered me from head to toe. "That's assuming the rest of the Council lets the wolves decide among ourselves."

She watched me without expression. "Carter might…"

"Don't." I refused to look at her, even in the mirrors, and concentrated on checking the hem and waist and back of the dress. I didn't want to look unkempt or rumpled at the wedding. It might be the last time I saw Carter, and I wanted him to remember me in the best possible light. Even if it was torture for us both.

"He wants to explain." She gripped her knees and continued on doggedly. "And you should listen."

"You don't understand."

"Maybe not exactly." She clamped her lips together as a seamstress knocked and ooh'd and aah'd over my dress, making a few final adjustments before she gestured for me to take it off. I complied, and once the seamstress disappeared with the dress, Natalia bulled on. Stubborn as a mule, that one. "But the thought of living a day without Logan takes my breath away. I can't function without him, Ruby, and I know it's worse for him. I can't imagine you would torture yourself by walking away from your mate. I just don't understand how you could do that."

"You're human," I said under my breath as I got dressed. "You're not an alpha, and you're not a wolf. For us, the mate and the pack take up parts of our soul, our heart. You can survive with one. That's enough."

"But why is only surviving enough?" She lurched upright and caught my hands, squeezing until my fingers cracked. "You shouldn't just survive, Ruby. Jesus."

"You don't get it, Nat." I pulled away and ran my hands through my hair. "And you won't. Ever. So let's talk about the party and what else needs to be done."

She gave me a dark look. "Don't shut me out just because you're being stubborn and miserable."

"I'm not." I hugged her and gathered my bag. "Put your clothes on so you can make me something delicious for lunch."

Natalia pulled on her jeans and scowled at me. "Don't act weird, girl."

She almost made me smile. As she led the way out of the designer's showroom, my phone rang. Carter. I hesitated, then silenced it and put it away. I wasn't ready to listen yet. I needed more time to figure out what Rafe and I were going to do. Then I could see if Carter fit in to those plans. My wolf didn't like it, wanted to stalk and chase him, but loyalty to the pack consumed her, as well. I forced myself to be cheerful as I followed Nat to the nearby apartment. At least I'd look damn good and go out in style.

chapter 20

The night of the party and Nat's surprise wedding, I spent most of the afternoon getting a manicure, getting my hair done, getting dressed in that gorgeous dress. I spent every minute of it second-guessing myself. I finally made a decision – what was best for the pack and for Rafe. And yet, my heart hurt just to think of it. My wolf mourned, but she understood.

I steeled my courage and had one of my wolves drive me to the warehouse where Evershaw worked. I didn't call ahead or give him any notice, but Todd assured me he was there. The younger Evershaw didn't ask any questions. Neither did my driver, though I caught her watching me in the rear-view mirror as she parked. I kicked open my door but took my time getting out, worried about falling on my face with wobbly high heels, and said, "Keep the doors locked until I come back out."

"Yes, ma'am." She gripped the wheel and stared straight ahead, as if she already knew what I planned to do.

The massive steel door opened for me before I even knocked, and Todd stood back to let me in. His eyebrows rose to his hairline. "O'Shea. You look…lovely."

"Thanks." I tried to sound like I meant it, and nodded to him. "Logan's party."

"Ah, yes." Todd smiled with half his mouth as he led the way through the empty halls. "I think our invitation was lost in the mail."

"I think Benedict might have forgotten to put a stamp on yours."

Todd laughed, shoving his hands in his pockets. "Does that still bother him?"

"You better believe it." I hesitated as Todd gestured at the door to his brother's office, and my stomach flipped until I thought I might barf all over the floor and the front of my dress. As I stared at the closed door, Todd leaned back against a nearby desk and folded his arms over his chest.

He watched me with a critical eye. "I was surprised you called. And that you wanted to talk to Miles."

"I'm pretty damn shocked myself."

He smiled more, looking down. "It would be nice if the packs got along."

"Yeah." I took a deep breath. "It would." I nodded to Todd and knocked on the door. "I'll work on that."

He opened his mouth to say something, reaching out to catch my arm, but then I heard Evershaw's deep voice from inside the office. "Come in." And I opened the door.

If I waited any longer, I might lose the rest of my courage. I needed to say my piece before I changed my mind.

Inside the office, Evershaw sat behind his desk, the entire surface covered in papers and cartons of half-eaten Chinese food. He frowned as he looked up at me, then the expression melted off his face. He eased to his feet. "Ruby."

My mouth went dry. He never stood up. Ever. It was a power play, always, to show that he owned the room and didn't have to get up for anyone. But he stood up for me, and called me by my first name. I cleared my throat to knock the words loose as I approached the desk. "Evershaw. Thanks for seeing me."

His eyebrows arched and he nodded at the chairs in front of his desk. "Sure. Have a seat. You look nice."

"Thanks." I perched on the edge of the chair, gripping my clutch so my hands wouldn't shake and clue him in to my nerves.

He rubbed his jaw and the graying stubble rasped against his palm. "I'm surprised you're here."

"Why?"

Evershaw shrugged and leaned back in his chair. "Technically, we still practice bride-napping. And since you walked into my den by yourself, I should just keep you."

My heart jumped to my throat but I refused to react. I kept my expression as blank as his, and prayed my voice didn't wobble. "That won't be necessary."

He glanced over my shoulder, toward the door, and I wondered whether Todd would overhear. Or if he waited with a bag to throw over my head. Bride-napping? But Evershaw didn't look concerned. "Oh?"

"I thought about your...proposal." The word tasted like ash. Business proposal, really. None of the magic, or love, or sentiment of Logan's proposal to Natalia. I talked faster, so I wouldn't change my mind. "And I accept, with a couple of conditions. BloodMoon pack remains under Rafe's control, and you drop the issue with the Council over there being a single pack in the city. SilverLine will not attempt to destroy or drive away BloodMoon. We can work out whatever power-sharing agreements need to be made, but I will leave BloodMoon and join you as alpha of your pack."

Evershaw didn't react at first, though he played with an extra chopstick as the silence stretched. Eventually, he cleared his throat. "Why?"

"Why?" I blinked and shifted my weight in the chair, uneasy. I hadn't expected him to question my decision. I didn't want to convince him to take me. It had been his idea. "Jesus, Evershaw, you were the one who..."

"Ruby," he started, then cut off and shook his head. He leaned his elbows on the desk and looked at me evenly. "Cut the bullshit. What the hell are you doing here when your mate is waiting for you?"

"Are you fucking *kidding* me?" My wolf snarled at the rejection, the insult that he would refuse us when we'd offered ourselves. I clenched fists against my thighs and wished I could shift and tear his throat out. But I couldn't ruin my dress, not with Nat's wedding in an hour. I struggled to breathe through my nose so I wouldn't pass out from sheer rage. "You, of all people, have *no right* to..."

"Why me, *of all people*?" Evershaw pressed his hands together near his chin and watched me. "What, because I'm an asshole? Because I made things a little tougher for Carter and for you?"

I lurched to my feet and threw my clutch on the floor. Picked up the chair I'd occupied and hurled it across the room, so it splatted against the fireplace and broke apart. I prayed I hadn't busted a seam. I wanted to break everything else in the office, including his face, as tears burned my sinuses and threatened to spill over. *I would not cry. Would not.*

"Because this was your idea. Your stupid fucking idea, and now —" I cut off and turned away so he wouldn't see me, just in case the tears broke free.

Evershaw, thank God, didn't follow me. He stayed where he was, and he sounded tired. As tired as I felt, as if every muscle hurt and every joint ached, and all he wanted was a warm bed. "Ruby, I proposed that deal before either of us knew you and Carter are supposed to be together. I'm not going to take another man's mate."

"I'm not going to be with Carter." I steeled myself and faced him, hands on my hips, and took refuge in the wolf's rage. "That's over. Done with. You two don't get to negotiate for me. I make my own choices, and this is it. This is my choice."

"It's the wrong choice." When I geared up to break something else, he held up his hands. A gold sheen rolled over his eyes. "Take a breath and sit your ass down, O'Shea. Before you break a leg in those ridiculous shoes."

"I hate you so much," I said, but part of me knew he was right enough about the shoes. I grudgingly sat, but I dragged the surviving chair away from the desk so I could establish my own territory.

"Join the club." Evershaw ran a hand over his short hair. "You're making a stupid choice. Part of it is my fault, but most of it is yours. You found your mate, Ruby. What the fuck else matters enough to walk away from that?"

"The pack," I said. "My pack. My pack matters. I've worked too hard to…"

"Bullshit. Packs come and go."

I rocked back in the chair as if he'd punched me in the chest.

Evershaw made a face, then yanked one of the desk drawers open. He pulled out a bottle of scotch and two glasses, and poured a healthy drink in both of them. He handed me one and finished his own before going on. "Look. I've led a couple of packs. Shit happens. Families break up. Some kid challenges you and you're having an off day. Or maybe you're just tired and hurt, and you walk away because it's not worth fighting for anymore."

I held the glass and sipped, wrinkling my nose as it burned my nostrils. But his words would have knocked me over if I'd been standing. "You left your pack?"

"Yeah, twice." His gaze slid away and for a moment the wolf looked out of his eyes. He shook it off and poured another drink. "And a couple of times the pack left me. So believe me when I say it's not worth giving up a mate for some bullshit pack."

"It's not that easy."

"It is." He shook his head, gold eyes searching my face. "Your mate is waiting for you to pull your head out of your ass, and he's been a hell of a lot more patient than I would have been. So go tell Carter you guys are meant to be, and get out of here before I vomit all over my desk."

I frowned as I looked at him. "And you'll give up this shit about a single pack in the city?"

He braced his hands on the desk. "No. It's a legitimate concern, which is why all the other alphas are entertaining the idea of a single spokesperson for each species. But I'm willing to table the issue until we have a discussion with both packs and the coyotes."

"Not the coyotes. They aren't going to make the sixty day deadline."

"I know." Evershaw sighed, and scrubbed at his face. "Don't remind me. Look, we meet some time next week and figure out how to make this work. Maybe the solution is a third pack, then we always have a tie-breaker."

A third pack. I stared unseeing at the corner of his desk, then shook myself out of my reverie. I didn't have time to sit around arguing with him. Although it was the first time he'd been a decent person. I kind of wanted a photo or something.

Before I could even suggest such a thing, Evershaw fixed me with an irritated look. "And don't look so fucking gleeful. I have reasons for everything I do. Just because I don't want you to be a miserable old wolf like I am does not mean I don't gain from it, as well. So go to the damn party and tell Carter he owes me one."

"We don't owe you anything," I said, just to make sure things were clear. "And we'll fight you if we have to, Evershaw."

"I would expect nothing less, O'Shea."

I wobbled to my feet, suddenly struck with a wave of emotion that almost knocked me back down, and I had to grip the back of the chair to stay upright. Carter. I could have Carter in my life, and maybe it didn't matter as much what the pack looked like. I had Rafe and Natalia and Carter, and they were enough pack for me.

As I concentrated on breathing through the maelstrom of emotion, Evershaw sighed. "If you're really conflicted, we could just fuck and you can get me out of your system."

"Seriously, I hate you." But I almost laughed as I said it. I gathered my strength and my skirt, and turned to go. "Thanks, Miles."

"Any time, Ruby." He sounded nonchalant, but I heard more scotch splash into the glass as I shut the door behind me.

Todd waited in the reception area, taut as a piano wire, and raised his eyebrows as I appeared. "Well?"

"We figured it out." I patted his shoulder as I strode past, feeling light as air even in those damn shoes, and headed for the exit. "We'll talk in a week and figure this stuff out. But I'm late for a party, so I've gotta run."

I even picked up my skirt and jogged for the door, shouldering open the heavy steel and scaring the bejesus out of my driver, who leapt out of the car and prepared to face whatever chased me. It wasn't an Evershaw chasing me, but a Chase pulling me forward. I didn't want to be late for Natalia's wedding, but the thought of Carter being there...being able to touch him, to be with him in public...I shivered.

I laughed and waved at her to get back in, jumping into the backseat. "Drive. Fast. The Chase mansion."

She did, but it wasn't nearly fast enough.

chapter 21

Carter almost didn't go to the party. The last thing he wanted to see was Logan celebrating his birthday, and he sure as hell didn't want to be in the room when his cougar matchmaker walked up to ask how all the dating went. Any answer he could offer would not be socially acceptable, or even polite.

But Logan insisted, and since the party took place in the ballroom at the mansion, Carter didn't have an excuse to stay home. He even wore the tuxedo Edgar left for him, though he grumbled and growled the whole time. He'd called Ruby a handful of times, and every time he got her voicemail. Even when Carter stopped by the bar to drop off the completed business plan, Rafe just shook his head when Carter asked how Ruby was doing. The other wolf alpha wouldn't talk about her, other than to say she was stubborn.

Carter waited as long as he could before heading to the party, but eventually Benedict dragged him out of his room and through the halls. He clenched his jaw until his teeth creaked as they entered the ballroom, and suddenly all of Logan's business associates surrounded them, wanting to talk investments, and portfolios, and plans. He tolerated it with the now-familiar mask over his features, even feigning a smile as one of the accountants cracked a numbers joke, and he understood better than ever why Edgar reacted – or failed to react – to some things. Carter could already feel numbness creeping through his heart.

And it almost cracked, when he looked up and saw Ruby walk in. The entire room hiccupped, she was that beautiful. Carter felt like someone punched him in the balls and the throat at the same time. He would have paid anything to be able to drag his eyes away, but nothing in the world could make him stop staring at Ruby. She stunned in a gorgeous black gown, tight in the right places and with plunging cleavage and no back at all. The smooth line of her shoulder blades made him groan into his wine glass.

She smiled at one of the bears, who looked out of place in a suit with a wild beard, but searched the room for something. Someone. His heart sank and he turned away, heading for the exit. It wasn't fair that she could look so content, so happy. He died inside, a minute at a time, and already she wanted someone else.

He barely got two steps before he ran into Edgar's chest. Edgar grabbed him by the shoulders, said, "Turn around, shit for brains," and physically forced Carter to face where Ruby stood.

Carter set his heels, like when they were kids and Edgar wanted to shove him into the pool to teach him to swim, and scowled. "Look, I'm not..."

"I know more than you. *Go talk to her.*"

The vehemence in Edgar's voice made Carter pause; Edgar never sounded that passionate about anything. So Carter stopped resisting and remained where he was as Ruby fought the crowd. She had to stop and shake hands with people, nodding to others, but her focus stayed on Carter. On him. It seemed like his heart started to beat again, as he wondered if maybe that joyful expression on her face had more to do with him than some other schmuck in the crowd. The lion rumbled and started to purr in anticipation. But the man didn't want to get his hopes up. He wouldn't survive if she rejected him again.

So he composed himself to neutrality as Ruby approached, and she flushed. She chewed her lower lip and rubbed her palms, shifting her feet as she looked at him. "You look handsome," she said, quietly. Almost shyly.

God, the lion loved it when she was demure. Shy and cautious, like they'd never seen each other naked, and he hadn't covered her in strawberries and eaten every one. Carter cleared his throat and tried to smile. "Thanks. You look beautiful, as usual."

The flush crept up her cheeks and the chewing grew more intense. He waited, part of him wanting her to suffer just a little, and it didn't escape his notice that Edgar and at least one of the bears kept the space around them clear of prying ears. Ruby edged a little closer and finally lifted her gaze to his face. Tears caught in her lower lashes, and his heart broke. "Look, Carter. I've been a jerk. I'm sorry. I shouldn't have blown up at you. I should have let you explain. I just…I saw you there in Evershaw's office and I assumed the worst of you, and I…"

"Don't," he said, and caught her hands. He wanted to hug her but knew the moment he did so, he wouldn't be able to stop holding her. The lion purred louder. "Ruby, you don't have to apologize. Please don't. All that matters is that you know I would never willingly undermine you or your authority, or try to get between you and your pack."

"The pack doesn't matter," she said, gulping, and a tear escaped to trickle down her cheek. She dashed at it but immediately grabbed his hands again. "I mean, it matters, but it doesn't matter as much as this. As us. You and me. Carter, we're — us. I can't imagine a future without you. I don't care about anything else. I just want to be with you."

His heart soared. He couldn't hold back any longer and reached for her, dragging her close in an embrace, and held her so tightly she squeaked. He buried his face in her hair, drinking in her scent and her warmth, and he didn't care that tears filled his eyes as well. "Always. Ruby, *always.* I'll never let you go."

Her arms tightened around him as she laughed, a bit teary, and her fingers worked into his hair. "Oh my God, Carter, I can't believe I almost lost you."

"You didn't," he said. He kissed her shoulder, her throat. He lifted his head enough to kiss her cheek and then his mouth pressed to hers, hungry and demanding, and her lips parted. Welcomed him in. Gave gracefully under his onslaught, and answered his passion with her own.

Carter drowned in her. His palm slid across her back, slipped in the open side of her dress and she made a hungry, needy sound against his mouth. Carter grumbled and his hand grew bolder.

"Okay, kids," a low voice said next to them, and through the fog of lust, Carter recognized Edgar's voice. "Don't make me get the hose."

He still remembered Edgar throwing buckets of water on Eloise and Atticus, so Carter knew Edgar would make good on his threat. Carter dragged his mouth from Ruby, struggling to breathe, but couldn't take his hands from her skin. She fixed Edgar with a glare that should have stopped his heart. "Edgar Chase, don't you…"

"They're about to start," Edgar said. He canted his head at the other side of the ballroom, where Logan picked up a microphone. "So you should be in the back with Natalia," and he pointed her toward a side room.

Carter, still dazed from the kiss and the warmth of her skin against his fingers, tried to decipher what Edgar meant. "Start what? Dinner isn't for —"

"Just get your ass up there," Edgar said, giving Carter a push, then dragged Ruby away and steered her to where Natalia apparently waited. Carter growled a little to see his brother touch her, but Edgar flexed and his higher rank silenced the lion.

Carter dragged his feet, looking over his shoulder to watch Ruby as she disappeared into the side room, and took his place on the dais next to Logan, Benedict, and Atticus. Edgar followed, patting his shoulder, and then Logan spoke into the microphone. "Friends, if I can have your attention for a moment. Natalia and I are grateful to have you all here with us today to celebrate my birthday. And some of you might be wondering why Nat isn't up here with me. Well, the reason is we have something else to celebrate — we're getting married. Tonight."

Applause erupted across the ballroom and cheers soon followed. Carter stared at his brother, but none of the others looked surprised. Logan hugged him, laughing. "Sorry, Carter. I didn't want to rub it in your face. But it looks like things worked out?"

Speechless, Carter slapped his brother's back and staggered back. A surprise wedding.

In a matter of minutes, the guests parted so a long red carpet could be unrolled. A door opened in the back of the hall and then Eloise and Sophia, both bridesmaids, walked the length of the red carpet. From the grumbles Benedict and Atticus made next to him, Carter figured those dresses had about as good a chance of surviving his brothers as Ruby's dress did at surviving him once he got her alone.

Sophia just smiled at Atticus, but Eloise stuck her tongue out at Benedict as she went to stand on the other side of the dais. Out of reach. Benedict even started forward a step, before Edgar's arm slammed across his chest and knocked him back. Carter blinked, distracted for half a second when he noticed Kaiser on the dais with them, wearing a suit and carrying a Bible.

And then Ruby appeared at the end of the carpet, and nothing else in the world mattered. His mouth went dry but his palms grew sweaty, and his heart thudded against his ribs. The rest of the people in the room disappeared. Her eyes locked on his, and Carter never wanted to look away.

Even when she took her place next to Eloise and faced back down the ballroom to where Natalia, resplendent in a white gown, appeared, Carter couldn't look away from Ruby. He managed to see Natalia in his peripheral vision, but Ruby was his world.

Kaiser officiated a short but very sweet ceremony, and Logan and Natalia read their own vows. There were tears and laughter alike, but more laughter, and Carter could not have imagined the depth of the love radiating from Logan and Natalia if he hadn't found Ruby. If he hadn't been able to kiss Ruby before the ceremony, it might have killed him.

And then the string quartet set up for the first dance, while servers in fancy uniforms circulated through the crowd with hors d'oeuvres and drinks. The open bar at the end of the hall did brisk business. Carter desperately wanted to drag Ruby away and find a private room where he could reacquaint himself with her curves. But she stood with Nat and Eloise and Sophia, posing for photos, and Benedict dragged him away to talk to someone about something. Carter barely listened, could not have repeated the man's name or how he knew the Chase family ten seconds after hearing it for all the money in the world. He only wanted Ruby.

It seemed only a blink but also an eternity of watching Natalia and Logan dance, avoiding the photographer, and trying to get enough food in his stomach so his stomach wouldn't growl when he finally got Ruby back to his room. And then he turned around and she was there, lips parted and begging to be kissed. "Carter Chase, will you dance with me?"

"For the rest of my life," he said, barely a breath of sound, and seized her hand, pulled her tight to his side. Almost tripped over his own damn feet trying to get to the cleared area in front of the string quintet. "Anywhere and everywhere. Even if there's no music."

"No music?" She laughed, and he loved the way her eyes sparkled. She looked happy for the first time in a long time, and he reveled in it. Wanted to bottle it up and roll around in it.

"We'll make our own music." Carter paused to kiss her, then twirled her around until her skirt flared out, and she laughed again.

The string quarter started playing the Etta James version of 'At Last,' slow and elegant, and Carter's breath caught. The perfect song, the perfect night, the perfect woman. Ruby felt it too, and melted in his arms. His heart soared. It took a moment for him to realize it, but she let him lead – didn't fight to turn them as he moved, didn't pull against his grip. She surrendered, easy and supple in his arms. She looked almost drunk, and he couldn't speak. It felt like a precious secret between them – trust. Total and complete trust.

He loved the song but rejoiced when it ended, because that meant he could hold her closer. Applause rose from the crowd, and Carter ignored it to capture Ruby's face in his hands so he could kiss her again. She broke away, breathless, and braced her hands on his chest. Looked up at him with eyes a little shiny from tears. "I should say good night to Nat. Can you wait?"

"Forever, if I have to." He brushed his lips across the back of her hand as Ruby drifted away, but before she got too far, he pulled her back for another kiss. "But sooner would be better."

She smiled and swirled away through the crowd to hug Natalia. Carter managed to drag his eyes away from her long enough to take his leave of Benedict and Atticus, and shook Logan's hand to congratulate him as he searched for Edgar.

Carter frowned as he spotted his older brother retreating to the exit, hands shoved in his pockets, and Carter opened his mouth to call out to him. Logan squeezed his shoulder, though, and said quietly, "Let him go."

Carter cleared his throat and shook his head. "Will he ever be okay?"

"I hope so." Logan took a deep breath, and then turned Carter so he could see where Ruby and Natalia hugged and cried and laughed. "Let me worry about him. You've got someone else waiting for you."

Ruby looked up, gaze smoldering, and Carter's desire sparked. His lion grumbled in anticipation, and he walked away from Logan without looking back. Ruby laughed as he stalked closer, and she retreated a few playful steps. He caught her, drew her to him, and kissed behind her ear before he growled, "You're coming with me. Now."

She watched him from underneath long lashes, and her fingers trailed down his chest to toy with his belt buckle. "And here I was hoping I would come first."

He kissed her again before saying, “Only if you’re good,” then patted her butt. He captured her wrist and made a beeline for the exit, all of his focus on getting to his bedroom before his lion took over.

chapter 22

The way he looked at me made my skin prickle and my stomach clench, and the hard strength of his body next to me on the dance floor almost made my knees give out. I could hardly concentrate enough to keep from tripping us both. Part of me wanted to stay for the party, but Natalia told me there would be many more parties, and after the last couple of weeks, Carter and I needed to celebrate. I wholeheartedly agreed, so barely an hour past the ceremony, Carter towed me through the empty halls of the mansion toward one of the far wings.

He didn't speak, just squeezed my hand in his, and when I cursed the high heels I wore for the third time, Carter fixed me with a dark look. "You're slowing me down."

I arched an eyebrow, heart fluttering at the challenge. "And what are you going to do about it, Chase?"

Without blinking, he picked me up and threw me over his shoulder, squeezing my ass. I slid my hand into the pocket of his pants and he jumped, arm tightening over my legs, and started growling. My heart thundered in anticipation as he shoved a door open, and then we were in his living room, then his bedroom suite, then he tossed me on the mattress and stared at me with such hunger, I knew immediately the dress was toast. Probably my bra, too.

Carter's eyes reflected pure gold at me as he shed his jacket and tossed it in the corner. But instead of springing on me and ripping away the dress, he eased into the wide chair in the corner. "Stand up."

I did, breath coming faster. I'd missed the command in his voice but the gentleness with which he treated me in public. I craved him. He got me addicted to him and I couldn't live without him. Carter watched me with narrowed eyes, feigning calm though I could hear his heart racing. "Take down your hair."

I eased a step closer, wobbling a bit in the heels, but reached into my hair and started pulling bobby pins out by the handful. Even with the hairspray and a few extra pins, it came loose in a long dark cascade down my back, and he made a hungry noise. I smiled, about to jump in his lap, but Carter held up his hand. "Wait. Stay where you are."

I wanted to touch him. I needed him to touch me. "Carter..."

"Strip for me." He leaned back in the chair until the darkness almost hid his expression. "The dress. Take it off. Slowly."

Lust surged and I almost couldn't breathe. My body felt full and over-heated and desperate, aching for him. But if he wanted a strip tease, I would give him a strip tease. The faster I turned him on, the faster I could pull him on top of me, pull him into me. Feel his hard length pressing into me, splitting me open. I moaned at the thought, and my fingers trembled as they brushed over my stomach. I'd never hated clothing so much in my life.

"Slowly," he repeated, voice mostly growl.

"Whatever you say, baby," I murmured, and turned slowly so he could see my back. He was an ass man, definitely. I fussed with the zipper on the side of the dress, looking at him over my shoulder to gauge his reaction, and let the dress slip from my shoulders. It slid a hairsbreadth at a time down my sides, revealing pale skin with excruciating slowness.

Carter made a hungry noise and shifted his hips in the chair, the evidence of his arousal obvious. I bit my lip to keep from smiling as I dropped the dress the rest of the way and let it pool on the floor at my feet. Then it was only silk thigh highs, a lacy thong, and a low-back bustier.

I bent slowly forward to pull at the heels, and again he snarled loud enough to make me jump. Carter growled. "Leave the shoes on. Face me."

I did. Desire flooded my core at the sight of him, on the verge of a shift just from lusting after me. He wanted me so badly he almost lost all control. I tried to look innocent, widening my eyes and biting my thumb.

His teeth flashed white in the dim room. "Take off the thong. Now."

I hooked my fingers under the scraps of fabric at my hips, and eased it down until it fell around my ankles. And I stood there, reveling in his attention, as Carter's hungry gaze raked across every inch of me. His fingers bit into the arms of the chair, and he lifted his hips in a slow thrust against the air that almost made me climax.

His chest rose and fell in deep breaths, coming faster and faster, then he managed to say, "Come here. Take off my pants."

"Whatever you want," I said, and his fingers tore through the buttery leather of the chair. I took the three stalking steps to the chair before I knelt and pressed myself between his knees. My hands shook as I undid his belt, then the fly, then I struggled to maneuver the zipper around his hardened cock. He helped, lifting his hips again, and I managed to slide his pants off entirely.

Carter, breathing hard, tangled one hand in my hair as he drew me in for a kiss – demanding , bruising. When he pulled back I nearly fell at his feet, seeing stars. But he released me and said, "The boxers. Off."

My nails raised goose bumps on his flesh as I ran my fingers up his chest and then back down to the waist of his boxers where the head of his cock peeked out. At some point he'd pulled off his shirt, but as I stripped the rest of his clothes away, I didn't care. I couldn't take the wait and touched his silky flesh, encircled him with my hand and slowly stroked the length of his erection. Carter groaned and his fingers worked into my hair. "I didn't tell you to do that."

"You didn't tell me not to," I murmured, and leaned forward to kiss the tip. I licked around the head and then up the whole length, squeezing the hardened flesh as I did so. I moaned as I took more of him in my mouth, and Carter cursed, hand tightening against my scalp.

Before I could do much else, he pulled me away and set me back on my heels. He breathed hard, eyes wild, and just as I thought he would throw me on the bed and teach me a lesson, he pointed at the chair. "Kneel here."

I straddled his thighs, trying to grind on him to satisfy my own aching need, but Carter held my waist to keep me from impaling myself. I wanted him so badly I held his shoulders and arched my back, hoping to distract him with breasts, but he held me tighter. He grabbed the bustier and tore it to pieces, casting it aside, and squeezed my ass. Carter pulled me close, until his cock was trapped between our stomachs and he could lick and suck on my breasts.

Fire consumed me as his mouth traced a heated path between my breasts and one hand slid under my thigh to tease my center. I jumped, desperate for more contact, but he held me steady and teased. His voice grew rough. "Don't move."

I growled my frustration and he chuckled, a warm rumbly sound. He stroked through the wetness gathering between my legs, letting me feel a hint of what was to come, as his cock slid between us. My head fell back as his teeth grazed my nipple, and it took every ounce of control I had not to tear free, grab his cock, and fuck him. Hard.

He kept teasing, letting the hard line of his cock ride against my slit until I moaned and writhed. Pleasure burned higher and higher with the slow tickle of his fingers and the soft stroke of his tongue, until I hovered on the edge. I just needed a little more. Of anything. Of him.

"Please, Carter," I said, hands tangled in his hair. "Oh my God, *please.*"

"Please what?" His grip tightened on my waist, hard enough to bruise.

A thousand replies flew through my head as I struggled to move against him, and none of them were sufficient. Until..."Please, love me," escaped, and I meant it.

He made a savage sound and lifted me, positioned himself, and plunged in with one smooth motion. I shattered. The world grew dark around the edges as every muscle in my body convulsed, and my core gripped him, held him tighter. Carter growled and purred at the same time, thrusting up at me even as his hold on my waist pushed me down. His hard length dragged from me, sparking tremors through my entire channel, and I cried out.

His thrusts grew jerky, uncontrolled, and his arms tightened around me until his face pressed between my breasts and I could lock an arm around his neck. I rode him through my climax, then another, and into his, until we both shook and panted and lay boneless in each other's arms. I rested my forehead against his as Carter leaned back in the chair, taking me with him, and his fingers traced my spine in a lazy journey.

Carter rested his head on the back of the chair with his eyes closed. "I will always love you."

I smiled against his cheek. Being in his lap, in his arms, was warm and safe. Exactly where I wanted to be. Protected when I needed, and supported always.

His hand drifted south so he could squeeze my ass and then smack my hip, though he didn't open his eyes. "Even when you're very bad and don't follow directions."

I wiggled in his lap and sighed with pleasure as his body stirred, lengthened inside me, and a wave of ecstasy rolled through me. I rolled my hips and tried to drag his mouth back to my breasts. "I wanted you to cut to the chase."

Carter groaned as his arms tightened around me, holding me in place as he thrust half a dozen times, then he withdrew, picked me up, and tossed me onto the mattress. He stood over me and I shivered with excitement. His voice grew deeper as he caught my ankle and dragged me to the edge of the bed. "What should your punishment be?"

My heart raced as I watched him, not sure if I was ready for the consequences of what I wanted to say. But I threw caution to the wind and let my arms fall onto the sheets above my head, laying fully exposed and open to him. "Surprise me."

He laughed, a deep and dark sound, and his hand slid up my leg to caress my thigh. "Are you sure?"

"No," I said, and closed my eyes. "But I trust you."

"Good girl," he murmured, and then he spent the rest of the night surprising the hell out of me.

epilogue

The bar rang with the clamor of patrons packed into the main floor. We hadn't been that busy in months. Our new chef slung orders left and right in the kitchen, and even Natalia, seated at the bar, looked impressed with the girl's attitude. Maybe there was a new challenger for iron chef. I pulled my last pint for the night, and folded my apron behind the bar.

Carter squeezed behind me to take my place, though his hands settled on my waist and I bumped my ass into his crotch just to get his attention. I did, enough that he almost jumped me right there, and Natalia covered her eyes. "Dude, you guys. Seriously."

I laughed and untangled myself from Carter's grip, though I jerked my chin at Logan, right next to her. "He doesn't mind."

"He doesn't get morning sickness," she said under her breath. "I can barely keep toast down and you guys canoodling around only makes it worse."

"Morning sickness?" Carter rolled his eyes and handed menus out to the few people who squeezed through the crowd at the other end of the bar. "It's almost midnight."

"It's morning somewhere," she said, and mustered enough dignity that I almost bought it.

But Logan finished his beer and hugged her against his side to kiss her forehead. "I'm with you, babe. Watching Carter kiss Ruby is like watching a kitten kiss a bulldog."

I looked at him, arms folded over my chest, and Nat looked horrified. "*Logan.*"

"What?" He looked at Carter, who was shaking his head and saying, "Dude" over and over, then at me. I wanted to rip his throat out, and it felt like the vein in my temple might burst. Logan scowled. "I meant fierceness, not looks. Jesus. Take a compliment, Ruby."

"Calling a woman a bulldog, for *any* reason, is grounds for an immediate ass-kicking," Eloise chimed in, as she and Benedict made their way to the bar. The half-gorgon leaned her elbow on the bar and waggled her eyebrows at me. "Want me to stun him for you? I could paralyze him. Just a little."

"Don't," Carter said, even though I was tempted. Carter kissed me again and patted me on the butt to send me on my way. "Not until after the Alphas Council. You both need to be…capable, if you're going to face off with Evershaw."

"Not a problem." I smiled at him as Rafe came out of the office, shrugging into his jacket. "The coyotes are not behaving themselves, so Evershaw is having to dig them out of trouble one hefty fine at a time. He's less and less interested in taking charge of all wolves and coyotes in the city. Hopefully at this meeting he'll retract the motion, and we can all figure things out."

"Besides," Logan said, breaking away from the scolding Natalia gave him. "We have bigger issues. The Auction is coming up and none of us want to see it go forward like it did last year. There are always a few cases of women offered against their will. The bears think they have a strategy for how to deal with it."

"A strategy?" Rafe snorted as he glanced at his watch. "Their strategy is usually to crush everything in sight. Period. End of story."

"They are not known for subtlety," Benedict said. The lawyer also checked the time, then scanned the bar once more. "Is Edgar coming?"

Conversation around us hiccupped, and I held my breath. Something hadn't been right with the Pride second-in-command since Nat and Logan's wedding, but no one would say exactly what. Logan just shook his head. "He needed a break. I'll fill him in when we're done. Are we ready?"

I nodded and turned to get my coat, but found Carter holding it for me already. As I shrugged into it, he wrapped the coat and his arms around me. Carter kissed the side of my neck as the rest of the family headed for the cars, Natalia talking loudly about watching teenagers make out, and Carter murmured, "I'll stay here to keep an eye on things.

If you call me when you're on your way back, I'll meet you at the apartment."

"We're really busy," I said, a little doubtful. "Wouldn't it be better…"

"I bought strawberries today," he said. He kissed the other side of my neck and I closed my eyes, let my head fall back on his shoulder. "And I think you're in desperate need of a hot bath. And probably a spanking."

I laughed, slow and lazy, as desire kindled. "Really?"

"Really," he said. His palm slid over my stomach to hold me tighter against his chest. His voice dropped and grew husky, a hint of a purr in each syllable. "Wear your high heels to the apartment. Leave them on. Clothes off before you walk into the bedroom. Hair down."

"Whatever you say." I wanted to ignore Rafe gesturing at me from the door, but he looked impatient. We couldn't afford to be late. I started to untangle myself, even though Carter's purr grew louder. He loved it when I mostly pretended to obey him. Of course, he loved it even more when I didn't. I shivered.

He leaned his elbows on the bar as I shouldered through the crowd, and I didn't have to look back to know he watched me leave. Just like I knew he would be waiting with a hot bath, the strawberries, the spanking, and at least a couple of surprises. I smiled as I got into the car and we headed for the Council building. Turned out I really enjoyed the surprises.

a sneak peak:

chasing the dream

Edgar hated everything about the resort from the moment he and Kaiser drove onto the grounds. The rest of Edgar's brothers, and most of the Council members and their fighters, waited on the resort grounds as the Auction got underway. But he and Kaiser had been chosen to walk into the Auction to determine the best time to act. Or if they even needed to act. The main ballroom was filled with giddy girls, their fathers and brothers and friends, and the eligible bachelors looking for a mate. Everyone there seemed eager to fall in love.

Edgar hated love. Hated everything about the earnest flirting, the coy glances, the crowds and expectations. It made his skin crawl. Logan had been apologetic, at least, about asking Edgar to walk into his worst nightmare, but that didn't make it any easier to wade through the giggles and gruff boasting. He reached for another beer.

Kaiser, looking almost presentable in jeans and a sport coat, raised an artful eyebrow as he scanned the crowd. "You need something stronger, Chase?"

Edgar made a face and waved away a well-intentioned butler with a glass, preferring to drink from the bottle. "If anyone else tries to give me their phone number or introduce me to their father, I will."

"Being a good-looking dude must be quite a burden."

Edgar shot the bear a sideways look, but couldn't quite tell if Kaiser was joking. The grolar bear — half polar bear, half grizzly — looked entertained more than anything as another girl, nervous and dressed entirely in pink, sidled up and asked if he was looking for a mate. Kaiser chuckled and thanked the girl but said he'd already found his mate — and then slapped Edgar on the shoulder with a wink for the girl. Her eyes went wide and she mouthed, "So sorry, you're very cute together," before fleeing back to her gaggle of friends.

Edgar gave the bear a sideways look. "Really, man?"

Kaiser's smile grew a touch as he shrugged, returning to his survey of the crowd. "You wanted to limit the girls hitting on you. Don't tell me you're uncomfortable?"

"I'm fine with however far you want to take this, man, but you're not getting past second base. No matter how much I drink."

Kaiser snorted and lifted his glass. "Right. So before we play a high-stakes game of 'flexible sexuality chicken,' let's find the organizers and get to the real problem."

"Great." Edgar tried not to scowl as he switched his empty beer bottle for a fresh one from a server's tray, and strode through the crowd toward the men they'd identified as the ones who put the whole thing together. They came from somewhere on the west coast, maybe California, although Edgar's favorite private investigator couldn't come up with much background on them. Even Bridger, one of the local loan sharks, could scarcely do more than provide grainy surveillance photos of the two men.

His teeth set on edge as he drained the beer and pasted on a false smile as he stood in front of one of the organizers. "Hey, mate. This is all well and good out here, but we heard there might be something more... intense available."

The man raised his eyebrows and offered a queasy smile. "I don't know what you're talking about."

Kaiser slid a folded hundred dollar bill into the man's jacket pocket, deliberate in his action. "I'm sure you do, friend. We're serious."

The organizer, a wolf, scanned the crowd behind them, then seemed to make up his mind. "Fine. Follow me."

Edgar shared a look with Kaiser and wondered where the bear got that kind of cash to throw around, but they followed in silence as the man strode away from the main ballroom to one of the reception halls on the other side of the main resort. The halls emptied the farther they got from the main event, until only a few servants and armed guards noted their passing. The organizer spoke quietly into a radio, then turned the corner to face a pair of giant doors, guarded by a handful of men and wolves.

He gestured at the doors. "You understand the rules?"

"Of course." Kaiser's lip curled with disdain.

The man eyed them both, then nodded to the guards, and one of the doors opened. Edgar strode in, fighting back revulsion as a wave of testosterone and anger and fear rolled over him, and immediately picked up another beer. Kaiser followed close on his heels, and the doors shut behind them. A crowd of about a hundred men filled the reception hall, with a tall dais on the far end. A man with a microphone called out a few jokes as someone cleaned blood off the mats in front of the dais, and an unconscious challenger was dragged away by some of the guards. Edgar's stomach turned over.

Kaiser frowned as they took up positions to observe from the wall near the dais, and Edgar studied the announcer, the bouncers, the guards, the escape routes, everything. The rest of the pride waited for the radio call and would storm in to mete out justice when needed. All he had to do was make the call.

The bear watched as one young man, goaded by his friends, shuffled to the front of the crowd, apparently convinced to take a swing at the next round of bidding. Edgar's lip curled in disgust and he nearly called his brothers in, just to end things before he had to watch the kid get his ass kicked.

Kaiser snorted, looking into his beer. "Owen calls that a 'hold my beer' moment. Something he got from the Corps, I guess."

"Oh?" Edgar feigned interest as he continued to scan the crowd.

"Yeah. Said that was the moment when he knew he needed to get his medical bag, or someone was going to jail, or something would end up on fire. After a couple of drinks, some kid would say, 'Here, hold my beer,' and then all hell would break loose." The bear gulped from his glass and set it on the tray of a passing waiter. "Every now and then you can feel it, can't you? That second right before your whole world shifts. Changes."

Edgar took a breath, ready to tell Kaiser he was full of shit, when a commotion brewed on the dais. Two bruisers dragged a girl up the steps. She looked partially drugged and certainly out of it, and probably starved as well. And pissed. Royally pissed. His entire world collapsed down onto her, the bared teeth and flashing gold eyes, a cold despair he recognized. Like part of her soul was missing and she'd spent her entire life searching for it, hoping to find it again. Except he knew it wasn't possible.

The announcer laughed into the microphone before waggling his eyebrows at the crowd. "A bit of a wild one, here. Young Ivy is a red wolf. No known defects or health issues, breeding status unknown. Ten thousand to start in the first round, an additional ten thousand for each subsequent round until only one fighter remains. Any takers?"

Edgar's heart climbed to his throat. She'd lost her mate. He knew it just by looking at her, knew it to his bones. Her breeding status should have been 'grieving.' 'Lost.' 'Lucky to be breathing at all.'

From his right, a surly older man with greasy hair raised his hand. "Aye, I'll stand a challenge."

"I'm in." This from a younger male on the other side the room, cruelty in the set of his jaw.

There was only one type of man who went looking for the kind of trouble that girl promised, and Edgar hated every son of a bitch who stepped forward to enter the challenge. The girl's eyes narrowed as she surveyed the crowd, then she lurched and threw off one of her captors. She almost freed herself from the second when the first jabbed a taser in her back and she went down in a boneless heap. The men laughed as they straightened, and Edgar started to growl.

Kaiser looked at him, eyebrows raised. "Problem?"

Edgar's eyes narrowed as he held his drink toward Kaiser. "Hold my beer."

The bear sighed as he took it. "Man, are you —"

Edgar didn't hear him, shedding his coat to toss over Kaiser's shoulder as he strode toward the dais. The girl deserved a chance to choose her own fate. She fought for herself when no one else would. Well, he'd damn well fight for her when she couldn't. Her mate would have been there, if he lived, but Edgar would do his best to honor the man's memory — and the girl's independence.

His voice came out more roar than human, and the crowd recoiled as he bristled. "She's mine."

One of the challengers, the one with greasy hair, scowled. "Who the fuck do you think you are? You fight like the rest of us."

Edgar pulled his dress shirt off, over his head, not bothering to unbutton it. He flexed, tattoos jumping across his back and down his arms, and the lion wasn't far beneath the ink. "I'm Edgar fucking Chase, and you better remember my name. Back off or regret it the rest of your life."

The man's eyes narrowed but he stood his ground. Maybe he couldn't back down, with so many witnesses. The young kid, on the other hand, and two of the other wolves who'd paid the ten grand to fight for her, backed off, hands held up in surrender. That left four serious contenders. Edgar bared his teeth and cracked his knuckles. The price jumped ten grand each round, as soon as a competitor dropped out, until only one man remained. As long as he could pay the price, he walked away with the girl. Edgar glanced at the dais, where the girl remained still and silent in a heap on the floor, then bared his teeth at the four men who faced him in a line.

They fought as a pack against the outsider, the lion, and would turn on each other as soon as he was knocked out of the fight. A cruel smile tugged at Edgar's mouth. They underestimated the lion. Underestimated the rage and pain and fury that boiled inside. A decade of hating life, of hating everything in the world, would spill out and over and those bastards would pay the price.

He flexed his shoulders and braced for the rush as someone rang a bell and the wolves surged toward him.

About the Author

Thank you for reading! I hope you enjoyed the City Shifters books. If you'd like to be notified of new releases, please join my mailing list by going to EEPURL.COM/BWQZ3X

Please feel free to email me directly at
LAYLARNASH@YAHOO.COM

or check out my website at
LAYLANASH.COM.

If you enjoyed the book, please take a moment to leave a review. I'd love to hear from you!

Thanks!
Layla

Also by Layla Nash

City Shifters: the Pride

Thrill of the Chase

Chasing Trouble

Storm Chaser

Cut to the Chase

Chasing the Dream

A Chase Christmas

A Valentine's Chase

City Shifters: the Den

Bearing Burdens

Bearing Hearts

Bearing Scars

Bearing Demons

Bearing Secrets

Other Paranormal Romance

His Bear Hands (with Callista Ball)

CPSIA information can be obtained
at www.ICGtesting.com
Printed in the USA
BVHW03s0200171018
530412BV00001B/56/P

9 781532 763281